DATE DUE   #2

MAR 0 1 2018	
SEP 2 3 2018	

The books in the Dragon Eye Series:
One: Dragon
Two: Hydra
Three: Phoenix
Four: Vixen
Five: Dracul
Six: Basilisk

Copyright 2014 by Finley Aaron and Henry Knox Press
Cover Design by www.designbookcover.pt

It is one thing to read about dragons, and another to meet them.—Ursula K. Le Guin

Chapter One

"Turn the wipers up faster!" Rilla shouts over the pounding rain.

"They can't go any bloody faster!" My mom is hunched over the steering wheel, cruising along at about 30 miles per hour, which normally wouldn't seem very fast, except we can't see anything through the deluge on the windscreen.

"We can't go on like this." Rilla, my sister who's older than me by about fourteen hours, takes her role as the eldest triplet very seriously, by which I mean she tends to boss everyone around. "We can't see where we're going. We might drive into the North Sea."

"We shouldn't be *that* close to the North Sea." Zilpha, my sister who hatched twenty hours after I did, is studying the big paper map unfolded on her lap. "Not unless we're even more lost than I thought."

"We've *got* to be getting close to the castle," Mom insists, which might be reassuring if she hadn't already been saying that for the last two hours, during which time we've zigzagged through most of the Scottish Highlands. "Look for Broadbottom Road."

3

"I haven't seen a street sign in miles." Rilla's in the front passenger seat, directly in front of me, her nose inches from the window as she tries to locate a sign.

"You won't find Broadbottom until we get on Invertinny Lane." Zilpha's beside me with the map, though she's mostly staring out the front in fear of oncoming vehicles—a justified concern, considering the road is essentially one lane wide, with occasional wider passing sections. This road was built for chaos on a good day. Considering it's raining, almost night, and we don't know how to get where we're going, I'm surprised we're still alive.

"Aren't we *on* Invertinny Lane?" Mom asks.

"No, that was Invernonny Hole." Rilla's aghast. "You didn't take *that*, did you?"

"Mom, please tell me you didn't take that." Zilpha's studying the map again. "That would take us in the opposite direction of the castle."

"I don't bloody well know which road I took. Why don't you tell me?" Mom's accent has been getting thicker the deeper we travel into the Scottish Highlands. It wasn't bad when we landed in Glasgow last night, but I wouldn't be able to understand her at all anymore if she wasn't saying the same things over and over—mostly cursing at the rain, the roads, and the other drivers. She comes by the accent both by blood (through her Scottish mother) and by upbringing (she spent ten years at a boarding school in northern England, just south of the Scottish border).

While my mom and sisters are arguing, I pull out my tablet computer with the maps I loaded in preparation for this trip, which I haven't been using because the battery is almost dead, and I don't have a charger adapter that works with anything in this foreign car. I'm trying to save it until we really need it, but if it means not spending the night on Invernonny Hole in the rental car with my mother and my two sisters, well, it's worth risking running out the battery.

Assuming we don't need it more, later.

4

I've already had to use it several times, ever since the GPS sent us around the complete *wrong* side of Loch Ness, which we didn't realize until we got to Drumnadrochit. When she saw the sign for the town, my mom screamed "Drumnadrochit!" over and over, making it sound like a bunch of curse words, and then swore off using the GPS altogether.

My tablet saved us that time and twice since. I'm starting to feel like a bit of a superhero, except that my powers are wearing down and my mission is far from fulfilled.

"Headlights!" Zilpha screams.

Twin beams have appeared out of nowhere in front of us. The oncoming car can't be more than thirty feet away, and there's nowhere for us to go because the road is only one lane wide, with bushes and puddles who-knows-how-deep on either side.

"Bloody, bloody, bloody," Mom mutters as she slams the brakes and squeezes over to the left side of the road, which is the side the Scottish drive on when they have more than a single lane, which right now we don't. The tires beneath me lurch as they leave the pavement, splashing into muddy holes.

I'm in the backseat of our tiny rental car, on the passenger side, which is on the left, directly above the holes. I stare past my sister Zilpha as the passing car zips by us on the right, hardly slowing down in spite of the tight quarters. If our vehicles hadn't been different heights, we'd have knocked mirrors.

Our car is no longer moving. Not forward, anyway. It rocks as my mom presses the gas, and the tires make an anxious spinning sound.

Futile.

"Are we stuck?" Rilla asks.

No, no, no. I do *not* want to be stuck on a narrow road in the Scottish Highlands, in the rain, in the dark.

The wheels splatter puddle mud as high as the windows, but the car isn't going anywhere.

"Wren, poke your head out and see what the trouble is." Mom says.

5

I've got a pretty good idea what the trouble is, and while I don't know what help it will be, I'd rather try to fix the problem now than wait until it gets completely dark outside. I open my door and find a couple of puddle-less spots to plant my feet. Then I study the tires.

Deep in mud. "Straighten your wheels out," I advise Mom through the open door, while I kick a bunch of loose gravel in front of the tires to create rudimentary ramps out of the holes. Then I climb back in the car. "Okay, drive straight out, slowly pick up speed, and then turn your wheel to get back on the road."

Mom mutters some incomprehensible Scottish words under her breath, but she follows my instructions. The tires stutter as they get hold on the loose gravel.

"Slowly!" I caution.

Mom doesn't panic or spin out. With a lurch, we're up, out of the holes. Another lurch brings us back onto the pavement.

To be honest, I'm surprised that worked. Car things are not my specialty.

That crisis averted, I return my attention to my tablet, where a reassuring blue triangle blinks at me from the screen. I try to ignore the cold wet seeping through my shoes. "We're on Willowick Road. Invertinny Lane is just up ahead. Keep going."

"How far?" Mom asks.

"I don't know. Look for a sign. It should be on the left." I switch the device off to conserve power. We've still got three more turns before we get to the castle. We might well need it again.

"A sign, a sign," Rilla mutters.

I join her peering through the glass. After a long bleary stretch our headlights reflect off a whitish slab. "What's that?"

Mom taps the brakes. "What's what?"

"There. Invertinny Lane—with an arrow."

"Is that sign on the *ground*?" Rilla studies it as Mom takes the turn. "Don't they have sign posts in Scotland?"

"This far out, you're lucky to get a sign at all," Mom admits. "Or pavement."

That last bit was under her breath, and I barely caught it, but the car's sudden rocking illustrates what she meant. I don't know if this road has ever been paved. Certainly not recently.

"Okay, look for Broadbottom Road." Zilpha traces the line on the map, the one Mom drew in based on the sketch the castle curators e-mailed us along with a line drawing of a turreted castle that makes it seem like the place we're staying for the summer was designed by an eight-year-old with a ball-point-pen.

In fact, Nattertinny Castle dates to something like the thirteenth century, which for some reason makes Mom think it's the perfect spot for us to spend our summer vacation. I am less convinced. To me, staying near one of the deepest lakes in Scotland (Loch Ness is 744.6 feet deep, a full 740 feet deeper than anything I want to swim in) is a supremely bad idea, and it's getting worse every minute.

It's also getting darker every minute. The sun hasn't quite gone down yet, I don't think, but with the heavy clouds and rain, it might as well have.

"Is that a sign?" Rilla asks.

"I saw nothing." I've been staring out my window, the same direction as Rilla, hardly blinking, ever since we got on this road.

"No, no, it was. Back up!" Rilla insists.

My mother, showing all the judgment of a woman who'd fly her three daughters to Scotland for the summer to celebrate their twentieth birthdays, throws the rental car into reverse and starts backing, never mind that she has no idea what's back there.

I strain to peer past the heaping luggage in the back window, but I can't see anything more than bulging canvas.

"There-there-there-there!" Rilla squeals, tapping on the window with her finger.

I look. There's a field running alongside the road, with barbed wire fencing and a big metal gate. In the middle of the gate there's a white sign with big black letters that says:

DANGER! No trespassing—live cattle!

And under that, in much smaller letters:

Broadbottom Road

And beneath that, in letters so small it would appear someone added them in by hand with a marker:

To Nattertinny Castle

"Hmm. Didn't the confirmation e-mail say something about a gate?" Mom asks.

"That's a *closed* gate." I'm staring at the locking mechanism, wondering if we can even open it without a key, and who's going to go out there in the rain to try, anyway?

"I was visualizing more of a wide-open gateway," Zilpha agrees.

"It says 'To Nattertinny Castle,'" Rilla insists.

Zilpha leans across me to see better. "Maybe they mean on down the road. Maybe there used to be an arrow pointing forward, and it got washed away, or something. Surely they don't intend for us to get out of the car and open the gate *manually*."

I've got my tablet back on, studying the map. Our little blue triangle is blinking at the junction of Invertinny and Broadbottom. "This is it," I admit, wishing it wasn't true. "This is the road. We have to go through that gate."

"Go open the gate," Mom orders.

"I can't. I'm holding the map." Zilpha waves the wide paper to validate her excuse, like she couldn't just put it down (although, in her defense, it *is* tricky to fold up again).

"I found the sign," Rilla points out, as though that somehow exempts her from any further responsibility.

"Wren!" Mom turns to me. "Go open the gate."

"Fine." I'm already wet, anyway, and I've turned off my tablet and stashed it back in my bag. I check for oncoming cars, then open the door and dart toward the gate.

The rain has let up slightly, so it's not quite so drenching, but still bothersome. The gate latch is this big slippery metal rod and clasp on the backside of the gate, so I have to reach around over the gate and get my sleeve soaking wet. The gate should swing wide open, but instead it thumps into a puddle, so I have to drag it back through the mud and rocks, and I'm trying to hurry but my legs knock against the metal gate with every step, and I'm soaking wet by the time my mom pulls the car through.

Then I close the gate behind us, even though it would be easier to leave it open and just get back in the car. But I'm pretty sure it was closed for a reason, and it did say *danger*, even if the danger is only cows.

Speaking of, the cows are standing about the field, getting rained on and watching me. These cows don't look dangerous at all, let alone enough to justify a warning sign with an exclamation point.

I dive back into the car.

"Ew, you're dripping wet!" Rilla pulls the paper map away from me as Mom drives over the lumpy road with a speed that's not nearly prudent, but will hopefully get us to the castle before it's completely dark out.

I ignore my sister and instead watch out the window, wondering what could be so dangerous about cows, anyway. Female cows and even steers aren't vicious creatures.

No, it's the *bulls* that are pure terrifying, though I don't see any of them around. A bull can weigh twice as much as a cow, all of it pure muscle run through with testosterone-fueled fury, armed with hooves and horns. A bull could trample this little car flat.

We're rumbling along the lane at a good clip when Zilpha starts screaming.

"Bull! Bullhorns! Turn around!" My sister's screams seem to pull their text straight from my fears. Or maybe my subconscious smelled it coming, I don't know. We dragons have an unusually keen sense of smell, though usually not so much when we're in human form.

Mom screams back, "There's nowhere to go!" as she throws the car into reverse and starts backing up.

A bull is charging us, our headlights glinting off his horns. It's this huge muscled thing, bigger than our rental car probably, with sharp horns that look like they could rip right through the doors and gore us.

Indeed, my mother is right. There's *nowhere* to go—the road is so deeply rutted it's a big jump to get up into the field. I don't know if a four-wheel-drive vehicle could make it, but this car certainly can't. The only passable direction is backward, and the gate isn't far behind us.

"Wren! The gate!" Mom screams.

"It's not my turn!" I point out, because there's no way I'm going back out in the rain, not with a bull charging us. Now the word *danger* seems insufficient. At the very least, they should have put more exclamation points on the sign.

"You're the only one who knows how to work the latch!" Rilla shoves me toward the door, which might seem sort of cruel except for the fact I'm not completely defenseless, and everybody in the car knows it. I mean, I may be a girl, but I'm strong—I'm about five and a half feet tall, of medium to larger build (even in human form, I'm muscular), and while I'm not wearing any swords right now, I'm still trained, as are my sisters, in not just swordsmanship but various martial arts.

Far more than that, though, I'm a dragon.

But then, so are my mom and sisters.

The bull is still maybe twenty feet in front of us when I open the door to run for the gate. But it's muddy here (a slippery, slimy mud) and I'm trying too hard to move quickly, besides which Mom hasn't completely stopped the car, so it's moving, too. As I attempt to shut the car door (I have to shut it or the car won't fit through the gate), the momentum of my arm's motion mixes in an unsettling way with the direction my feet are pointed, and I go down splat on my hands and knees.

This is bad.

The bull is way too close, maybe a dozen feet from the car and my screaming family. I have no choice. I'll have to change into a dragon, pluck up the bull, and carry it off into the hills some safe distance away.

I've no sooner made up my mind, and my fingernails are starting to lengthen to talons and turn blood red, the deep color suffusing my skin in a rush from cells to scales, when I hear screaming—male, guttural screaming, from just behind the car.

Chapter Two

I cannot allow myself to be seen as a dragon.

Even if I *could* get away with being seen as a dragon (which theoretically a person could explain away somehow, maybe, though I've never tried it and don't want to) I most certainly cannot allow myself to be seen *changing into* a dragon. It's completely, totally, and in all ways against the rules.

No one can know who we truly are.

No one can even know there are dragons alive in the world today.

Our continued existence depends upon it.

So I snap back into full human and spin around in the direction of the screaming, all in the time it takes the bull to charge two strides closer.

There's a Scotsman—a wild-eyed, red-haired bearded man with an enormous broadsword, which he holds over his head as he runs screaming toward the bull, which is only a few feet from the front of the car by now.

The red-haired guy is still screaming as he brings the blade down over the bull's muscular neck. The head falls into the puddled road and the animal's body sort of stumbles forward and slumps over it.

And the dude is still screaming. I don't think he's even stopped to catch his breath.

He must have amazing lung capacity.

But now he stops screaming and turns to me, his wild red hair settling into dripping streaks across his forehead. He smiles. "Ilsa Melikov?"

"That's my mother." I point to the car, where my mom and two sisters are still cowering from the rain, dangerous bulls, and screaming Scottish swordsmen. "I'm Wren. Wren Melikov."

I'm staring at the Scotsman. He's dripping wet, his big red beard hanging past his navel, which is most noticeable because he doesn't have a shirt on. Judging from his shoulder-to-waist ratio, which is impressive, I must admit his choice of attire, or lack thereof, is not entirely unpleasant from my perspective, though I imagine he must be cold.

He's also wearing a kilt. Not the typical plaid kind, but a dark charcoal gray utility-type kilt, and black leather boots that stretch up to his calves, with bulky pewter buckles and straps all over them.

All in all, an imposing bull slayer.

He extends one hand to me. "I'm Eed. Eed Cruikshank."

As I shake his hand, a number of things occur to me all at once. One is that his name is probably Ed, not Eed, even though he pronounces it *Eed* with his Scottish accent. Another is that his last name, Cruikshank, means knob-kneed, which he is. He'd be well over six feet tall, except his knees are bent askew, so he's hardly brushing six feet.

And besides his knobby knees, his hands are kind of funny, too—calloused and thick-knuckled, but I don't so much see them as feel them as he shakes my hand quickly and apologizes.

"I was headed up to git the gate fer ye." His Scottish accent is thick, even thicker than my mother's. "Sorry I didna make it in time. Didna expect ye to be so quick."

Then he points with his sword toward the bull carcass, which is bleeding into the puddle, making it look like a lake of blood in the light from the rental car's headlamps. "Sorry if this bugger skeered ye. He won't trouble ye anymore."

"I didn't mean for you to have to kill him," I apologize. Bulls, I'm sure, are expensive creatures, though they're not worth nearly as much without their heads attached.

"Nah," Ed makes a guttural sound with his throat, dismissing my concern. "He was on his last warning. I'll pull him out the road and ye can drive on up to the house, just around the bend there." He points with his sword again, this time down the road in the direction we were heading.

13

I clamber back into the car, closing the door as my mother cruises forward again, past Ed, who's moving the carcass off the road.

Hmm. Now that is particularly strange.

I know a thing or two about bulls, having eaten many in my time. They're big, much bigger than cows. This one was probably two thousand pounds before Ed lopped his head off.

But Ed isn't dragging it by its legs or chopping it into smaller pieces for easier removal. He's got it over his shoulders and is running through the field, carrying it off.

"Did you see that?" I ask, even as the rain falls more heavily, cloaking the fields from sight.

"What?"

"Did you see Ed carrying the bull?" I ask again, more specifically this time, only to have my question met by silence.

Rilla is consumed with the tricky task of folding her map.

Mom is busy fiddling with the wipers.

Zilpha looks back at me blankly. "Ed?"

"The Scotsman with the broadsword, who saved us from the bull."

"I didn't catch his name." Zilpha shrugs.

She looks tired. We're all tried from traveling—flying out from Bozeman yesterday morning, to Denver to Newark to Glasgow, which between the time changes and the flight times took until this morning—and then driving slowly up the Highlands all day today, taking the roundabout scenic route so Mom could see things she hadn't seen since she was a kid at boarding school.

But now, in addition to being tired, I'm also feeling a little suspicious.

I know my mom's always talked about bringing us to see the place where she grew up, but this isn't technically that place at all. We're in Scotland, not England. They may be on the same island, but they're not the same place.

14

And my dad and brothers aren't with us. Yes, I know somebody needs to stay home and watch over our village in Azerbaijan and be the dragon protectors and keepers of the fire and all that, but the fact that all the girls are on vacation and all the boys staying home seems a tad odd, especially when you consider that I wasn't keen on coming on this trip (since deep lakes terrify me), and my brother Felix has always said he wanted to visit Scotland.

But he's not here, and I am.

Now I'm starting to think maybe there's a reason for that, and I study my mother as she guides the car down the rutted lane to the castle, which is a looming fortress jutting straight up into parapets and battlements and all those castle things we've missed seeing for the last six years while we've been living in the states.

My mom glances my way, perhaps a bit self-consciously, and flashes me this tiny, apprehensive smile.

She's up to something. Oh, she is *so* up to something. The woman can't hide anything. You can always read her face as clearly as any book—figuring out our birthday presents was only ever as difficult as guessing the right thing and then watching her face for confirmation.

Right now, Mom's face says she's guilty of plotting something.

But what?

I'm going to have to corner her and rattle off guesses until her face gives it away. But before I can do that, we'll have to get situated in the privacy of our suite of rooms, because most of my ideas have to do with us being dragons, which isn't something anyone outside of our village is supposed to know.

The headlight beams flash across three men who exit the castle and approach our car. These are the guys from the castle website—handsome Scotsmen in ties and tweed jackets, none of them shirtless or kilted or carrying a sword. None of them Ed.

My mom stops the car under the shelter of the port cochere. We tumble out of the car and the men make their introductions—Malcolm, Magnus, and Angus Sheehy, the curators of the castle, who run the place like a vacation home bed-and-breakfast. Magnus and Angus are brothers. Malcolm is their father. His wife Blair is in the kitchen right now, heating up a late night tea for us.

The castle has been in their family for centuries.

I listen politely and shake hands as needed, but I'm listening to the subtext, filling in what I hear with what I already know of our plans.

We've reserved a suite of rooms for six weeks this summer. The Sheehys occupy another portion of the sprawling castle. Ed lives above what used to be the stables. He'll be around shortly to unload our bags and park our car.

Mom's asking about activities now, tourist spots and seeing the sites, and here it is, the bit I've been waiting for. Indeed, she's arranged it with Malcolm that his sons, who are both single and handsome and look to be twenty-something, will be on hand to escort us and guide us and provide any other services as needed.

I should have known!

She's trying to set us up with these guys, isn't she? It's never been any secret that we're expected to marry other dragons someday. In fact, the very existence of our kind depends on our finding proper mates and bearing young, and all that.

I look Magnus and Angus up and down. Proper mates, hmm? How does my mother know these men are dragons? Or is she only guessing?

The fact that the castle has been in their family for centuries might be a clue, since dragons only started dying off in the past thousand years or so.

Tracking down our extant peers could theoretically be accomplished by digging through history and finding the last known dragons, then rooting about to discover whether they have any descendants left. And since dragons traditionally lived in remote treasure-filled palaces and mountain fortresses, a castle such as this one would be the logical place to find dragons.

Not that we've ever actually found any dragons that way, not that I know of. To my knowledge, we're alone on the earth, save for a couple of arch-enemies who are obviously not viable romantic partners.

But perhaps my mother has found some after all. That will be a relief to my sisters. Zilpha, in particular, has always been eager to marry. She's spearheaded many a historical research project, trying to drudge up potential suitors, though we've never found a single one. And Rilla has said more than once she'll gladly marry and do her part, as long as she can finish her degree first.

I, on the other hand, am hedging my bets that in a world where dragons are nearly extinct, we'll be lucky enough to find a mate for Zilpha, and maybe even one for Rilla, too. If Angus and Magnus are the two, that's perfect. There's not a third. I can be blissfully free of any entanglements, as I've always wanted to be.

While I'm musing about all this and my mother's making plans for Magnus and Angus to give us a tour of the castle tomorrow, Ed approaches us through a small door in the castle curtain wall. He's put on a tweed jacket, but he's still wearing his kilt and boots, and his flame-red beard looks wild.

And he smells like roasting meat.

My stomach grumbles, reminding me I haven't had anything to eat since the fish and chips in Fort Augustus, which we stopped for on our way through the first time, *before* Drumnadrochit, so that was several hours ago.

"Ed." Malcolm pronounces it *eed*, too. "Bags." He gestures with his head.

Ed nods. "I put the bull on the spit."

Malcolm looks annoyed at Ed, which I can see because I'm off to the side from the others. But when Malcolm turns back to my mother, he's smiling graciously. "In addition to tea, we have fresh flame-roasted beef. I don't suppose you ladies would be interested—"

"I'd love some," I offer before my mom can open her mouth to turn him down. Besides the fact that Ed killed the bull in large part to save me from the mad animal, I'm hungry. And from what I can tell from the scent still clinging to Ed, the meat is going to be delicious. Some people don't like bull as well as steer, because the testosterone supposedly makes the meat wilder or gamier or something.

I like it better that way.

But then, I'm a dragon.

Ed's opened the rear hatch and is pulling out our bags, which are heavy and numerous. The four of us barely managed to carry them all into the airport, but Ed's stacking them up on his shoulders like a block tower. I half expect them to topple off any moment.

Ed turns to face us. "I kin show ye to yer rooms." He doesn't even sound out of breath. But then, if he carried a two-thousand-pound bull with no problem, our luggage is nothing. It all confirms my suspicions that there's something peculiar going on with this place, Nattertinny Castle, and Mom's plans for us to summer here. I can't recall ever hearing anything about Scottish dragons having freakishly strong lackeys, but it wouldn't at all surprise me. In many ways, it makes sense.

I follow Ed.

My mother and sisters hang back a little behind me, almost as if they're afraid Ed's going to drop the luggage and we'll all go tumbling down like so many dominoes. But Ed doesn't even pant as he steps through the vast stone foyer and up the broad staircase.

This place is cool, if a bit spooky. There's an enormous chandelier hanging down from the second-story ceiling high above us. It looks ancient even though it's lit with light bulbs instead of candles, like maybe it was retrofitted to electric light. But even with all those bulbs, the massive room is dark, the polished wood stairs a deep mahogany finish, the stones dusky gray, the corners shadowed.

The damp of outdoors has followed us in, or perhaps has always been here. It's cold and clinging, as thick as mist. Invisible, but as tangible as the scent of roast meat wafting back to me from Ed, as real as the scent of the lavender soap I packed in my bag, which got bumped as it tumbled onto the baggage claim carousel at Glasgow, which has been leeching out lavender scent ever since.

My lavender and Ed's meat scents mix in the air as he navigates the hallways ahead of me. I follow like a hound on the hunt, chasing the smell through cold corridors, until light fills a doorway ahead of me, casting Ed's burdened silhouette into dark relief.

"Here ye are, then, Miss. This'll be yer sittin' hall." Ed places our bags on waiting luggage racks with a gentleness the Glasgow baggage handlers would do well to study. "There's bedrooms 'ere, 'ere, 'ere, and 'ere. Bathrooms en suite." He flicks on lights as he speaks, reaching through doorways and bursting the darkness, obliterating the shadows with the flip of a switch. "Is there anything else ye be needin'?"

"Mr. Sheehy mentioned fire-roasted beef?"

"Aye, that'll be ready any time. It's in the courtyard."

"Can you take me there?" The corridors we passed through were a complicated maze. I can hear my mother and sisters approaching through the halls, drawn to the light. Much as I love them, I'd like a break from their presence. Besides, I'm hungry, and fire-roasted beef is one of my favorite foods.

But more than that, I'm curious about this place and Ed. Neither are normal, but I need to observe more before I can figure out just what's different about them.

"I can. Show ye a shortcut, even."

"Perfect."

Chapter Three

I follow Ed through the doorway just as my mother and sisters round the corner to our hall. I explain where I'm headed. Mom and my sisters seem more interested in unpacking than eating, which is fine by me. I'm more interested in eating than changing out of my wet clothes because, let's face it, in this weather, I'll probably get soaked again the minute I step outside.

Ed leads me through a hallway and down some stairs, and just when I'm starting to think the cold stones of the back hall are a little too reminiscent of a dungeon, I smell fresh wood smoke and roasting beef, and we step outside.

There is the bull, gutted, skinned and sizzling, over an enormous fire whose flames are a warm welcome after the rain.

"Yum." I reach my hands out toward the fire, but it's a huge blaze, so I don't have to get very close to feel the warmth.

"It'll be a mite wild-tasting, Lass. Not such as yer used to, I'm afraid."

"I like it that way. Is it ready?"

"Only if you like it rare." Ed didn't blink when I said I like wild meat. Most people, when I say something like that, look at me like I don't know what I'm talking about, or like maybe I'm bluffing.

Ed looked, if anything, impressed.

I can't help smiling. "Rare's my favorite."

"Mine too. Ye can wash up there and grab a plate." He gestures to a hand pump. We're in a stone courtyard surrounded by the castle on three sides and a stone curtain wall on the fourth. Wide eaves provide shelter from the rain around the three sides, but where the bull is roasting, the courtyard is open to the endless dark clouds above.

Fat sizzles from the meat, hitting the fire and sending sparks dancing toward the starless sky.

I wash up, taking the time to brush the mud and gravel from the knees of my jeans. Then I splash water on my hands again and grab a plate, turning back to the fire to see Ed cutting meat from the sizzling carcass, using a broadsword and a long-handled prong that looks more like a pitchfork than a kitchen utensil. He's got his jacket off again, which I guess makes sense when you're that hot.

I mean, working close to a hot fire.

The *fire* is hot. Obviously.

I'm standing here, plate in hand, watching him work, the muscles in his back rippling (did I mention he didn't have a shirt on under that jacket? He didn't) as he carves through the juicy beef. Maybe a vacation in Scotland isn't such a bad idea.

"Here ye are."

I step forward and he lowers an enormous cut of beef into my plate. It's probably three pounds, more like a roast than a steak. "Perfect. Thank you." I carry my plate over to a table under the eaves, where utensils are wrapped in cloth napkins in a basket. Sitting, I slice off a big bite, and let the moist deliciousness sit on my tongue for a second before I chew and swallow.

Glancing back toward the fire, I notice Ed has sawed off a chunk of meat for himself, but he's eating it in the far corner of the courtyard, his back to me.

"You can join me," I offer, feeling isolated. Who wants to eat such a fantastic meal all alone? And Ed saved me from the charging bull. He should not have to stand in the corner. Besides which, I want to learn more about him, the Sheehys, and this castle. I'm not going to shout that conversation across the courtyard.

"I'm not supposed to eat with the guests." He looks startled, maybe even a bit guilty. "I don't have the good table manners, and all."

"I thought your manners were exceptional when you saved me from getting gored by the bull." I'm not going to push the issue, but he doesn't strike me as a total caveman. I saw the way he handled our luggage. He's considerate and careful, if brutishly strong.

With a palpable measure of hesitation, Ed settles his steak onto a plate and sits opposite me, off to the side, near the far corner of the table, where it's darker, further away from the light of the fire. Still, the table's only about eight feet long, so he's easily within talking distance, especially since the rain is falling like thick mist now, almost soundlessly, and the stone walls reflect our voices back to us.

For a few moments, there's only the clink of knives and forks against plates. The beef is fantastic, and I was hungry. Conscious of my tablemate and his claim to crudeness, I peek his direction and watch him saw through his meat.

Indeed, he is a bit clumsy. There's something wrong with his hands. I'd noticed it before, briefly, in the rain. I still can't see exactly what's up, but his fingers appear to be gnarled and stiff, more fitted to beheading the bull with a broadsword than slicing bites of meat with a knife. Still, he manages, and looks my way after swallowing.

"Ye here to see the loch?"

An involuntary shudder moves down my spine at the reminder of the fathomless depths of the famous lake nearby. "I—I suppose."

Curiosity sparkles in his green eyes, and he leans closer my way. "Yer not afeared of the monster, are ye? Ye don't strike me as the fearful type. Didna even seem afeared of the bull."

How can I explain to Ed that neither bulls nor monsters scare me half us much as that deep water, where anything could be lurking, waiting to pull me down? Memories of what happened last summer threaten to surface, but I submerge them with a question. "Is there a monster? Nessie?"

Ed makes a face. "Don't call him Nessie. He's not a girl."

Okay, now I'm curious. "So, the Loch Ness Monster is real?"

Ed shrugs noncommittally and saws off another hunk of his steak. Still, the twinkle in his eye says he knows something.

I press for answers. "Have you seen it?"

"It?" Ed corrects me. "*Him.*"

"Have you seen him?" It occurs to me that this local man might have insights into the matter that others, even the monster-sighting tour boat operators, may not have. Especially if he lives in a castle with dragons, as I suspect. We monsters tend to stick together.

"Would ye like to have a look for yerself? I could take ye out on the loch tomorrow."

Me? Go out on that crazy deep lake?

No, no, no, no.

"Yes," I answer in spite of myself. I'm afraid. Terrified, really. But more than the fear that makes me want to flee in the opposite direction, I want answers.

Are sea monsters real?

If so, that might explain what attacked me last summer.

Worse than the fear, is not knowing whether my fear is justified, not knowing my enemy or even being sure if I have an enemy outside of my own head.

Ed and I make plans to meet in this courtyard tomorrow at nine in the morning, then Ed finishes his steak moments before my sisters and mother arrive with the Sheehy men. Blair Sheehy, Malcolm's wife, is right behind them, carrying a tray with tea.

Having finished my steak, I accept Blair's offer of tea with thanks, and stand nearer the fire with the warm cup in my hands while Ed serves steaks to my mother and sisters. He tends to the roasting meat, rotating the spit to his satisfaction before slipping quietly away through the door in the curtain wall.

I watch him with curiosity. If it weren't for his knobby knees and gnarled hands, he'd be the finest specimen of Scotsman I've seen on this trip, even accounting for the football team we saw go through the airport dressed in suit jackets with their kilts.

24

I can't help wondering how old Ed is. He doesn't look any older than I am, save for his thick beard which makes him seem older. But at the same time, something about him seems ancient. Maybe it's the broadsword or the kilt or the centuries-old castle around us. I want to learn more about Ed.

My sisters, however, seem fully enthralled with the Sheehy brothers, and my mother announces their plan to tour the castle in the morning, then drive around the lake in the afternoon. She implies I'll be going with them.

I inform her otherwise. "Ed's taking me out on the loch."

My mom looks shocked, probably because I've been avoiding deep water ever since I escaped from whatever it was that may or may not have attacked me in the Caspian Sea last summer.

Malcolm Sheehy clears his throat. "Ed doesn't usually interact with guests."

"Is it okay? I mean, he's safe, isn't he?"

"Oh, Ed's one of the safest men I know, probably the best person in the world to take you out on the loch. He just…doesn't usually interact with guests. Or people. Much."

"Ever." Angus coughs, the word half hidden under a snicker.

Magnus chuckles.

Their father gives them a stern look, and their mother leaps to her feet to offer another round of tea.

I accept the refill with thanks, and sip it slowly, mulling this newfound information. True, Ed was reluctant to interact with me. He'd made it sound like that was the Sheehys' rule, though. Not his personal preference.

Being naturally reclusive, myself, I wouldn't be surprised if Ed used the Sheehys as a mask to hide behind. If anything, the fact makes me feel more comfortable around him. My sisters and the Sheehy brothers can be sociable, while Ed and I slink off and be reclusive together.

Even my mother seems to resign herself to the fact. She's a wise one, my mom, and she knows her daughters well. No doubt she's reached the same conclusion I have—that if there are two Sheehy dragons, and the two of her daughters interested in getting to know them better are also the two who hope to find a dragon mate, then there's no reason to force the introverted third daughter to be sociable.

The day has worn on Mom, as well, and she finishes her steak quickly, excusing herself to return to our rooms. Since my sisters are lingering, spending more time chatting up Magnus and Angus than eating, I figure this is my chance to find out what Mom's up to. She's more likely to confess if it's just me, especially if she's already given up on hooking me up with anyone.

Between the two of us, we find our way back through the halls and up the stairs to the warm light that shines from the open door of our suite. I close the door behind us and, not knowing how much time we'll have before my sisters return, I waste no time asking questions.

I try the indirect approach first. "Nattertinny Castle seems really cool. How did you find it?"

"They have a website. You saw it."

"But how did you find the website?"

Silence. And utter lack of eye contact as my mom suddenly becomes absorbed in rooting through her bag.

I press further. "Do you know the Sheehys?"

"Hmm?" Mom picks up the bag and all but sticks her head inside, muttering something about her contact lens case.

"Isn't it with your other toiletries? Did you put it in the bathroom?" I'm reminded that my eyes are pretty itchy, too, after long plane rides with my contacts in. We dragons have startling jewel-toned eyes, so when we're out among other people, we wear color-dulling contacts to keep our true identities a secret. I slept in mine on the last plane.

Itchy, indeed.

"Oh, that's right. Thanks." My mom heads through one of the bedrooms to a bathroom, which is spacious and sparkling white with Carrera marble, and well-lit with chrome fixtures, which gives the room a much brighter feel than the other parts of the castle we've ventured through.

Mom plucks out her contacts while I stand behind her, jealous of the relief her eyes must feel, but unwilling to abandon this conversation until I've gotten answers.

Considering how much my eyes itch, I'm no longer willing to take the indirect approach. "Are the Sheehys dragons?"

Mom fumbles the contact case, spilling lenses and lens solution onto the marble floor. "Oh, bloody hell. Wren?"

"What?" I crouch down beside her to find the fallen lenses. Her amethyst eyes look guilty. "Why would you think...?"

"Why else would you bring us here? We're turning twenty this summer. Older than you were when you married dad."

"That was a long time ago." She plucks up a lens and rinses it carefully over the sink.

"Not yet twenty-two years," I note matter-of-factly, finding the other lens and holding it out to her, standing patiently behind her, meeting her eyes in the mirror. "So, are they?"

"I dunno." Her Scottish accent is plenty strong. "They're contenders. The strongest contenders I know of in the world. But I don't know if they're dragons and I can't figure out how to ask, without, you know—"

"Giving away that we're dragons?"

"Aye."

Chapter Four

"So, what makes you think they're dragons? And how sure can we be?" I've got my own suspicions, but I want to hear my mother's side.

"It's a long story." Her contacts out, she follows me back to the sitting room where my bags still sit, untouched, where Ed left them.

"Tell it to me. I've got time." I search for my contact lens case.

"If I tell you, you've got to promise not to let on to your sisters."

"Why not?"

"For one thing, I don't want them disappointed if I'm wrong. You know how much Zilpha wants to marry. She's a romantic at heart, but more than that, she wants a family of her own and children. If she thought these Sheehy boys were dragons, and then found out they weren't, she'd be heartbroken. Rilla, too, but less so. I don't mind telling you, because we all know…" she gestures emphatically with her hands, but doesn't speak the words aloud, as though saying them might somehow bind me to a fate she'd rather I avoid.

I have no such qualms. In fact, I'd love to be bound to this fate. "I don't want to get married," I announce aloud. I've found my contact lens stuff, and pull the itchy things from my eyes. Ah, sweet relief. We can see just fine without them—in fact, we dragons have exceptional eyesight. If anything, the contacts make our eyesight worse, especially when we've had them in too long, which is my excuse for not seeing the sign to the castle earlier. My bright red irises look back at me from the mirror above the mantel, glowing with vibrant color.

My mom makes an exasperated face. "Why don't you want to marry?"

I sigh. She's asked me this question before, and I've thought about it. I can almost put it into words, but I don't want to offend her. "I want to be me."

"You don't stop being yourself when you marry."

"But I want to be *me*. Wren. Alone. Master of my fate, hero of my own story. Ever notice how many movies, when they get married, that's it? The story ends when they get married, or fall in love, or whatever. I don't want my story to end."

"It doesn't end. You just live happily ever after."

"As someone else. Your name changes. You change. I don't want to change." I scowl. She's gotten out of telling me her story. Time to fix that, and quickly, before my sisters show up and she refuses to tell it at all. "Enough about me. The Sheehys. What makes you think they're dragons?"

There's a fireplace at one end of the sitting room, and a handy stack of wood beside it. Still cold in my damp clothes, I head toward the stone mantle, while Mom settles into one of the two sofas that flank the hearth.

I pile wood in the fireplace, check to be sure the damper's open, and open my mouth as though to yawn, instead letting loose a torrent of flames onto the dry wood, starting a crackling, cheery fire.

Sometimes I love being a dragon.

"Mom?" I turn to find her looking sheepish. "The Sheehys?"

She begins reluctantly. "You know how my mother and father met, right? My mother, your grandmother, Faye Goodwin, is from Scotland. She was a dragon, one of the last of her kind. She saw her friends and family hunted nearly to extinction, and she began to despise what she was. So when Eudora, a dragon from Siberia, sent a rumor through the dragon world that she could change dragons into humans, my mother went to her."

I settle into the sofa opposite my mom, cringing slightly, because I hate this part of the story. My grandmother was tricked by Eudora and nearly killed. Fortunately my mom spares me the details.

"My father, Elmir, had spies watching Eudora. He learned Faye was there and went to rescue her. Until that time, he'd never met her. Didn't know anything about her, hadn't even realized there was a female dragon anywhere in the world until it was almost too late. But as he tried to nurse her back to health from her injuries, they got to know each other and fell in love. I am their only child, hatched from the lone egg she laid before Eudora attacked again and the yagi killed my mother."

I nod, knowing well the story from this point forward. Mom had no idea she was a dragon until she was eighteen, almost nineteen, and the yagi hunted her down. My father protected her and brought her back to her father, Elmir, her only living parent.

Mom continues, "At the time when my father and mother met, my father only knew of very few remaining dragons, nearly all of them male. He asked my mother if she knew any other dragons."

This is new. I've never heard this part of the story, and I'm instantly intrigued. "Did she?"

"She said there was a dragon who lived near Loch Ness, a male dragon. Long before, they'd discussed marriage, but since she didn't want to be a dragon anymore, she didn't want to marry him. She wanted to be something else. She rebuffed his advances and refused him."

I'm on the edge of the sofa now, riveted. There is another dragon in this world? We're not alone? It's the most amazing feeling. Incredible, really. And since dragons don't grow any older once they've reached the age of maturity, there's every chance the dragon is still around, an eligible mate for one of my sisters. "What's his name?"

"She didn't say."

"She *didn't say?*" I'm gob smacked. This is the most important information anyone could have told me, perhaps ever, and my grandmother simply failed to mention it?

"She was injured. Dying. They had a lot on their minds. It didn't seem important then. Besides that, you know how it is— we don't reveal our identities to anyone, especially back then, when dragons were actively being hunted to extinction. Sharing his name meant putting a mark on him, targeting him for death."

"But grandpa wouldn't have hurt him."

"True, true. But when you're in the habit of keeping a secret, you don't spill it the first chance you get."

"But we need to know his name. Zilpha wants so much to marry. She wants it more than anything. If dragons are going to continue to exist for another generation, we need to know the identity of the man—"

"I know, I know. That's why we're here. We're going to try to find him. If he's still alive he should be around here somewhere. Dragons don't leave their treasure hoards unprotected."

Her words remind me of the advantage we have of being a family, instead of one dragon all alone. My father and brothers are watching over our village, our treasure and our people. In the same way, when my father made the perilous journey home with my mother nearly twenty-two years ago, her father, my grandfather Elmir, watched over both his and my father's villages, which are neighboring kingdoms among the Caucasus Mountains of northern Azerbaijan.

If my mother's suspicions are right, there's a dragon around here somewhere. Maybe even in the same building with us. "And Nattertinny Castle? Why'd you pick this place?"

"It's the oldest castle in the region that's been continuously occupied by the same family. On top of that, in the old Scots Gaelic, the *nat* prefix was associated with dragonflies and a feminine variant of the word *dragon*. And *teine,* which transliterates into the suffix *tinny,* means *fire.*"

I put the words together. "Dragon-fire castle?"

My mom smiles. "And conveniently, they let out rooms."

31

For a few seconds, I study the fire, my very own dragon fire in the dragon fire castle. I'm thinking Mom is pretty savvy, after all, for bringing us here. But then I realize something troubling. "Mom?"

"Hmm?"

"You said Grandma Faye knew of one other dragon, but there are four Sheehys, and two sons." I'm trying to rectify what she's told me with what I know. See, dragons are immortal creatures, insofar as they live forever, unless you kill them. When we're in dragon form we're pretty tricky to kill. When we're in human form, we're nearly as vulnerable as anyone else. But no matter which form we're in, we only age until we're young adults, and then we just hang out looking twenty or so for centuries.

So if my grandma knew another dragon, even three hundred years ago, he'd still look like he was my age today. He'd still be a perfectly viable romantic partner, even if he was hundreds of years old. I know that may seem strange to people who are only humans, but it's perfectly normal for dragons.

Mom frowns. "I've thought about that. It's possible she only knew of one of the sons. One may have been born since. Or she might have known Malcolm. Perhaps he found Blair later and married her and had the two sons."

I mull these possibilities. "How old do you think Malcolm looks?"

"He looked younger on the website than he does in real life." She sighs.

"I'm not going to argue, he's in great shape, plenty handsome, but I don't know that I'd say he looks forever twenty. His sons look twenty, but they also look younger than he looks."

Mom throws her hands into the air. "Who knows? We can't say. Perhaps, if you get to be hundreds and hundreds of years old, perhaps it starts to show. Perhaps he wears makeup to look more appropriate to his age."

"Perhaps." It *is* a possibility. My mother is guilty of reading articles about 'make-up mistakes that age you,' just so she can make those same 'mistakes' in an effort to keep people from thinking she's one of my sisters. And I can tell the difference when she uses them.

Mom rises to her feet. "Why don't you change out of your damp clothes and get to bed? We won't solve all the mysteries of the universe tonight."

I rise as well. "Indeed, we won't." But tomorrow is another day, and perhaps, with Ed's help, I might solve a mystery or two.

*

In spite of my jet lag, I awake early the next morning, eager to learn whatever I can about the questions that have been plaguing me. Are sea monsters real? Are the Sheehys dragons, or is there some other dragon somewhere in the vicinity who's been stealthily hiding out for centuries, ever since my grandmother rebuffed his advances?

I follow the scent of bacon downstairs and find Blair cooking up breakfast in the vast kitchen that adjoins a smallish dining hall.

"What can I get for you?" She asks with a smile.

"Is there any more of that beef left over from last night?"

She dismisses my question with a wave of her hand. "Oh, no. Ed took care of that. I've got fresh bacon, though, and blueberry scones coming out of the oven in three minutes."

"Scones and bacon sound great." I smile, even though I can't help wondering what Ed did with the meat. It was good meat. I hate to think it may have gone to waste.

"Coffee until then?"

"I'd love some."

My sisters arrive as I'm eating. They're excited about spending the day with Magnus and Angus, and they don't mind that I won't be joining them. I can't help wondering if they suspect who Magnus and Angus might really be, or if they're just keen on romping through the highlands with a couple of handsome fellows. Knowing Rilla and Zilpha, it could be either.

Finishing my breakfast, I grab my jacket and camera from my room and follow the back hall shortcut to the courtyard. I'm early, but Ed is already there, shoveling the coals from last evening's fire into a metal tub. When he sees me, he self-consciously grabs a t-shirt and tugs it on before greeting me.

"Lemme just finish this here, and we'll be off."

"Take your time. I'm early."

With a few more hefty scoops he clears the fire pit, then hefts the ash tub. "Follow me."

I follow, grateful he's not the chatty type, glad he's invited me on this excursion in the first place. The Sheehys seemed surprised by this offer, which makes me feel like I'm being given an exclusive glimpse of the loch most tourists would never get to see. At the same time, I can't help wondering about the breadth of his knowledge of local monster lore. Last night, he made it sound as though he knows some things about the Loch Ness Monster.

Maybe, just maybe, if there's a dragon in the area, maybe he knows a bit about that, too.

But I can't think how to bring up the subject. I'm not a chatty person and neither is he, so we make our way in mostly silence to an old pickup, and rumble down the rutted path of Broadbottom Road, which is not nearly as broad as the name suggests.

When we reach the gate I offer to hop out and open it so Ed can drive on through, and he accepts my offer with gratitude, and then we're through and away, in a matter of minutes efficiently covering in reverse the path it took me and my mother and sisters so long to decipher in the rain the day before.

And before I'm quite sure I'm even ready to be at the lake, I catch glimpses of its mirror-like surface reflecting the morning light, and then Ed turns off the main road onto a pair of ruts I wouldn't have thought passable by vehicle—which, even driving upon them, I am still not convinced are passable by vehicle.

And then he rolls to a stop by a small wharf with a handful of fishing boats docked alongside it, none more than sixteen feet in length, most hardly more than rowboats. These are private recreational vessels, not tour boats. Ed leads me to a dinghy equipped with both oars and an outboard motor.

I hesitate, looking first at the tiny craft, then at the vast loch. To be honest, when I was floating on my back in a vessel made of my own wings, last summer when I was attacked on the Caspian Sea, I was bigger than this dinghy. We grow in size when we take our dragon shape.

Ed hops into the boat, which lurches from his weight, sloshing in a less than reassuring manner. He extends one gnarled hand up to me. "Come aboard?"

I glance back the way we came. Along the shore the water seemed clear, with rounded rocks protruding up from the surface, and submerged rocks still visible through the water amongst them. But here, where the water is only slightly deeper, I look down into darkness, a kind of blackness that could hide anything, darker than the halls of Nattertinny Castle at night.

"The water is dark. I can't see the bottom," I inform Ed while I clutch my camera close to my body, not taking his proffered hand, not moving any closer to the boat.

"Aye," he acknowledges. "'Tis the peat content. Loch's thick with it. Can't see more than five feet down. Black as night down there, 'tis."

His words are not reassuring, but something about his matter-of-fact tone and the transparency of his admission remind me of what Malcolm said the previous evening—that Ed is one of the safest guys a person could venture onto the Loch with.

Ignoring the dark, bottomless water, my eyes fixed on Ed's face, I take his waiting hand and step into the boat.

Chapter Five

The tiny vessel lurches, rocking unsteadily, and I hold tight to Ed's hand, my eyes pinched shut.

"Ye goin' to be all right, then?"

"Yes. Fine." I chirp, forcing my eyes open. I paste a tight smile to my lips and give him an impatient look, as though he should get on with casting off. Like I'm not the one holding us up.

"I'm goin' to need me hand then."

Only then do I notice I've got his poor bent fingers in a death grip.

I release them, realizing after all human contact is lost how much difference his support had made in my state of mind.

Ed reaches for the rope that moors us to the wharf. The boat lurches with his movement.

I grab his arm, which is the nearest thing to me. Okay, it's more like his shoulder that I've grabbed with both hands—one handful of bicep, one handful of deltoid, possibly trapezius. I don't know. I just know I can't let go.

He looks at me, concern showing clearly on his face in spite of the beard that covers its lower half.

Not wishing to acknowledge my fear or draw attention to the possibility that my viselike grasp of his shoulder is anything out of the ordinary, I flash him a reassuring smile. "Hi."

"Hi there, aye." His Scottish brogue is smooth. "I need to untie the boat."

"Okay." I don't let go of his shoulder. I can't.

"Gonna need the use of me arms, then."

"Of course." I nod as though I understand completely. For a second, I start to relax my hold.

Ed moves, perhaps as much as an inch or two, in the direction of the moorings.

The dinghy lurches.

I grip his shoulder harder.

"Wren?" Ed says patiently.

"Yes?"

"Last evenin', I coulda sworn I watched ye leap out the car right in front of a chargin' bull. And I thought to myself then, 'this is a woman who's not afeared of anythin'.'"

"Charging bulls are not as scary as boats."

He eyes me patiently. I appreciate that he doesn't bicker, or dissect the logic of my position.

"I can take ye back to the castle." He straightens slightly.

"No! Oh, no, I'll be okay. I'll be fine." I ease my grip slowly, transitioning to letting go. "I really want to go out on the lake."

"No, ye don't."

"But I do. I need to. I have to find out if the monster is real."

"Is it the monster yer afeared of?"

"Not the monster." I'm looking in his eyes now, dusky green eyes with a hint of blue, and I'm trying to sort out what it is, exactly, that I am afraid of. "Not the boat, and not the lake. Just the water—the deep water. I'm afraid of the parts of the lake that are too deep to see, and what might be down there that could grab my legs and try to pull me under."

"The monster wouldn't do that."

"It wouldn't?"

"There's been nearly a hundred recorded sightin's, and never a one in which anyone was ever attacked or even approached. Most of the time, the monster was either oblivious to being observed, or tryin' to get away from the people."

"He's more scared of us than we are of him?"

Something like empathy fills Ed's features. "Aye."

Slowly, carefully, I open my fingers, releasing his shoulder from my grip, though my palms are still touching his shirt, and he's still turned, facing me, his eyes locked with mine. It's the eye contact that's keeping me from looking at the lake and freaking out again.

I can do this. I have to do this. If Ed takes me back to the castle, I'll never convince him to bring me out on the lake again. And I can't imagine a tour boat operator being so patient with me.

This is probably my only chance to get answers, whatever they may be.

Ed doesn't move. "I'm goin' to untie the boat now," he explains smoothly, his whole body frozen in place like a statue. "I'll reach past ye to the moorin'. Boat might rock, but I promise ye, it willna tip over. Ye be safe. Ye ken?"

I nod one slow, solitary nod. And then I watch, breathing measured breaths in and out, as Ed unties the boat.

He smiles at me once we're loosed from the dock. "Ye can have a seat there."

The boat has a couple of bench seats. We're standing at the rear, near the outboard motor. There's a seat in front of us—a plank spanning the width of the craft—and another closer to the front of the boat.

I lower myself onto the plank and swing my legs around so I'm facing the front. Only then do I realize something terrifying. If it wouldn't involve movement to reach Ed from this position, I'd grab his arm again. Instead I squeal, "Ed?"

"Aye?"

"There's a window in the bottom of the boat." And there is. It's a huge glass panel occupying most of the center section of this tiny ship, so that what almost seemed slightly safe a moment ago, is now a window into murky darkness and everything I fear.

"'Tis water-tight. Nothin' to be afeared of."

We sit in silence while I try to believe his words. I'm clutching the bench seat with both hands and staring down at the window to my fears. Ed's standing above me, trying to decide if he's crazy to take me out onto the lake, or if he should just haul my quaking self back to the castle. He doesn't voice the question aloud, but I can feel it radiating off him as he looks at me.

"Ye want to go out on the loch?"

"Yes, please."

"Okay." He sits beside me on the plank and grabs an oar. "You want to row one, or you want me to row both?"

"I can row." Surely it will be good for me to have something to do other than staring through the glass bottom of the boat at the murky water below.

With a few instructions and a bit of bumping about, we get the boat pointed out onto the lake, and put some distance between ourselves and the shore. I take long slow breaths and try not to make it obvious that I've pressed the side of my leg against Ed's leg beside me. I need the human contact. It's soothing.

It's a cool morning, midweek, and the lake doesn't appear to have much, if any, traffic. Certainly not in the vicinity where we are.

Loch Ness is a long, narrow lake, if you're not familiar with it. Long, narrow, and crazy deep. It occupies a fault line, or something like that. A ripple in the earth filled with water and cold and monsters. The east and west sides are relatively close together, a pretty stable mile apart for the length of it, but the lake is well over twenty miles long, so that I can't see either end of it any better than I can see more than black water through the window below.

Just as Ed and I are getting our rhythm down and I'm starting to think we make a fine rowing team, he announces were in a good spot and can stop rowing. The boat glides gently along the lake, which is calm and mirror-smooth, save for the dying ripples of our wake.

"Now what?" I ask after a long silence and no sign of any monsters.

Ed shrugs. "Some people fish. Some just sit and enjoy the stillness. Some might want to explain why they're afeared of being pulled under."

I look uneasily his way.

He raises an eyebrow, not so much in question, but in open invitation for me to share.

40

He's not pressing me for answers, even though I nearly cut off the circulation to his arm with my clamped fingers earlier.

Maybe it's the stillness of the lake or Ed's patience, or the hope that he might take my side in spite of the fact that my own family failed to believe me. For whatever reason, I sort my thoughts, arranging the story in my head first to be sure I can tell it without giving away that I was a dragon, in full dragon form, for the duration of the events I'm about to relay.

Okay, I can do this.

"I nearly drowned last summer."

His eyebrow, which had gone back to a relaxed position, darts up again, willing—even curious—to hear more.

"We were swimming in the Caspian Sea. I'm from Azerbaijan, which is on the western shore of the Caspian Sea, and we've vacationed on the Sea every summer for my whole life. My sisters and I have been going to school in the United States ever since we started high school, six years now, but we always go back to Azerbaijan in the summer."

"You're triplets?" Ed clarifies.

"Yes." I don't go into detail. We've always referred to ourselves as *triplets,* and my sisters even claim my birthdate for legal purposes, so we don't raise any eyebrows, but technically we're not triplets the way most people think of triplets. We're more like littermates or hatchlings from the same clutch.

Dragons lay eggs, just like any other reptile. My sisters and I were born from the same clutch of eggs, but technically Rilla was hatched the night before me, and Zilpha the day after me. Likewise, our eggs were laid over the course of a few days, too.

But I don't tell any of this to Ed. I just nod and keep on with my story.

"We're triplets," I confirm. "We have an older brother and a younger brother, and we've always summered on the Caspian Sea. I've floated and fished and gone swimming there more times than I can count. I never felt unsafe and never had a problem.

41

"But then, last summer was a busy summer because now that we're in college we have a lot of other things going on vying for our time, and we didn't get much time at the lake, only a couple of days. I wanted to soak it up, you know? Spend every moment I could on the water. So the first afternoon when we got there, I went out on the lake and didn't worry about coming in when it got dark."

What I don't explain to Ed was that I was fishing, in dragon form, floating on my back in a boat made of my own wings, with a basket on my belly and my tail drooping down in the water, a glowing lure to bait the fish, which I then reached down and grabbed out of the water with the claws of my bare dragon hands when they swam near.

I've done the same thing more times than I can count, eating fish, tossing them in my basket, being lazy and basking in the pure joy of being a dragon and virtually weightless in the water all at once. It's a freeing feeling, one I'd always relished, until it got turned on its head and became something to fear.

"And then what?" Ed prompts me, and I realize I've been silent for a while.

"I'd floated pretty far from the others, I guess. I felt safe. I wasn't worried. And then, with no warning, something grabbed my legs and pulled me under. For a second I thought maybe one of my siblings was playing a trick on me, only they've never done that before, and whatever it was that had me didn't let me go or start laughing or anything. They pulled me down deeper toward the cold water, and I fought them and fought them until I thought I'd never get away. My lungs were burning. I've never been so terrified."

"But you got away?"

"I scratched and clawed and got loose and made my way to the surface." What I can't tell Ed is that I used my talons, horns, and the spikes on my tail to fight off my assailants. Then I flew back to shore, well above the water, back to my family in a frenzy. But I do tell him the other part, the very important part. "I got back to my family and told them what happened, and my dad and brothers went out to look. But they didn't see anything. Didn't find anything. They went out the next two days. Nothing. No sign of anything. It was like it had never even happened."

"But, weren't you scratched or bleeding?"

I shake my head. Being a dragon at the moment, I was pretty impervious to spears or knives or claws. But that doesn't even matter so much because of the nature of the attack. "It wasn't teeth that got me, or claws or talons. It was like something grabbed hold of me with its hands."

"Not a human?"

"How could it have been human? They pulled me down. They never rose above the water. They didn't breathe air."

"They? There were more than one?"

"There had to be at least two or three, maybe more." I'm trying not to be overwhelmed by the memories, hands clutching my arms, my legs, my tail. "My brothers came up with a theory that I'd floated into a thick patch of seaweed and got tangled up and it pulled me down."

Ed is looking at me earnestly, and I'm staring right back into his face, waiting for his verdict, for him to laugh off the attack and tell me my brothers are probably right, that I'd freaked out myself and my family all because I got in over my head with a tangle of weeds.

But he doesn't say this.

"Did you see anything? You're sure it wasna scuba divers?"

"I couldn't see anything. It was getting dark out. The sun was going down—it was a glare of red across the surface of the water, mostly darkness, just enough to stun your eyes and make it more difficult to see. But I *felt* them."

"What did they feel like?"

"They had heads. Smooth heads. And arms that were flat like paddles, but with hands at the ends. They had bodies. I kicked their bodies. No scuba tanks. No tubing or gear. If they'd had scuba gear I could have pulled out their mouthpieces and sent us all up for air." I've described them now in as much detail as I gave my family, and I fully expect Ed to lecture me about the fact that nothing in the world fits that description, that I had to have misunderstood my enemy.

That my fear overpowered my good sense.

That I was wrong.

Instead he asks, "Can you remember the place in the lake where you were attacked?"

"Yes. Vividly." I can picture myself rising up from the water like a shot, hovering there above the sea for a few seconds, gasping for breath and staring down for some visual confirmation of the enemy I'd just fought. But there was nothing more than a swirl of water in turmoil, a few bubbles, and then still, lapping waves.

Then I'd looked to shore, spotted my family, and flown like a streak back to them, only to receive a lecture about flying too high in dragon form before it was fully dark out, my glow too bright and boats too close, risking that I might be seen. I think it was perhaps their need to justify their lecture, their anger at my overreaction, that kept them predisposed against my story once they failed to find any sign of the monsters I described.

But Ed gives me no lecture and shows no predisposition against my theory. Instead, he seems ravenously curious about these water monsters. "Can you take me there?"

I'm completely thrown by Ed's request. "You want to go to the Caspian Sea?"

He nods. "To the spot where you were attacked."

"It's a long way from here. My father and brothers searched and found nothing."

Ed doesn't even blink. "I study sea monsters, livin' close to the Loch, as I do," he explains. "Ye might even call me a sea monster expert. If there's anythin' down there, I want the chance to look."

I'm panting a little from the excitement of telling my story, from the fear it roused in me. Much as I'd love a sea monster expert to validate my story and tell me what really happened, it's a long journey. I don't want to waste Ed's time. "The creatures probably swam away. It's a huge body of water. A sea, not a lake. They could have gone anywhere. I don't know how you'd ever find them. It could take years."

"Years I have in abundance." He tells me solemnly. "What I don't have is answers or evidence. Do you think you got tangled up in seaweed?"

"I know I didn't."

"Then take me there, and I will find the monsters that attacked ye."

Chapter Six

Tiny waves, the wake of a distant boat, lap against our dinghy as I stare at Ed, pondering my response. On the one hand, I'm grateful, so very overwhelmingly, wordlessly grateful, that he believes me. His simple acceptance of my story has restored a part of my heart that was crushed by my family's disbelief.

I could hug this man.

But there is also the simple fact that the monsters that attacked me, if they are real (of course they are real—do you honestly think I, a dragon, was nearly drowned and defeated by *seaweed*?) are dangerous on a level Ed, for all his sea monster expertise, cannot begin to understand. To put it in perspective: the Caspian Sea monsters nearly killed me when I was in dragon form, thirty feet long with horns and talons and armored scales.

Ed is just a guy. He's a pretty big guy who can carry headless bulls on his shoulders at a running clip, and tote precarious stacks of luggage up stairs without getting winded, but he is still. Just. A. Guy.

The Caspian Sea monsters will obliterate him.

There are few things I am sure about in this world, but this I know: I do *not* want someone as nice as Ed, a guy who saved me from a charging bull, the only person on earth who believes me about the monsters—a guy I could hug—obliterated by ruthless sea monsters.

On the other hand (and the lapping waves die down to nothing, returning the lake's surface to its usual mirrored self while I ponder it) I could fly Ed there on my back over the course of a couple of days, he could search the sea, and we could be back in under a week. Logistics-wise, this could happen.

There's just that whole part about Ed getting obliterated by sea monsters. That's my sticking point.

So finally, after Ed's been more than patient, waiting for me to respond, I explain to him, with a gravity in my tone that I hope captures the danger of his proposal, "The sea monsters tried to kill me."

"Aye," Ed acknowledges, his tone almost apologetic.

"I mean, they almost *did* kill me."

"Are ye worried for me safety?" Ed looks surprised, maybe even amused by this notion, as though no one has ever been worried for his safety before. Considering his skill with the broadsword last night, probably no one has. Still, I can't imagine him fighting the sea monsters with a broadsword.

"Yes. I'm worried for your safety. It's dangerous."

"I'm a mite bigger and stronger than ye are."

I have to turn my head away to hide my laughter. Ed may think he's big and bad, but I'm a freaking dragon. I am so much bigger and badder than he is.

"What's that?" He peers around me toward where I've hidden my face. "Have ye been tellin' a joke?"

I sober quickly, because it occurs to me that, with his knock knees and funny hands, he might have been teased as a child. And I don't want him to think, even for a second, that I'm laughing at him. "No, not a joke. I'm just trying to think. How do you intend to find the monsters?"

"Well, ye don't seem keen on me goin' in the water. I have a set of underwater cameras, see, on account of me bein' a sea monster expert livin' near Loch Ness, and all. Sea monster investigatin's a major local industry, ye might say. So I could use the cameras to look, first, if it would make ye feel better."

"Cameras. Okay. Cameras seem safe." I'm slightly appeased by his plan, except that he said *first*. "And then what?"

"Then, depending on what I find, I'd go underwater."

"You'd go underwater?" I repeat, my lungs constricting with fear. "That's the part of the plan I don't like. It's dangerous."

"Yer afeared I'll be pulled under?"

I nod.

47

"I can hold me breath a good long while. Does that help?"

"It depends. How long can you hold your breath?"

His eyes twinkle with something like mischief. "Wanna test me and see?"

"Sure."

To my surprise, Ed stands, peels off his shirt and starts unbuckling his boots. He is taking this challenge to his big strong manliness very seriously.

I'm confused. "You can't hold your breath with boots on?"

"I'm goin' in the loch."

"You can't go in the loch. It's freezing cold."

"It's nay so bad." He's got his boots off now, as well as his socks, so that he's stripped down to just his kilt. Honestly, if I'd have known I'd see this much fine shirtless kiltedness on this trip, I'd have been more eager to visit Scotland. Then he stands on the bench and executes a graceful dive into the loch, surfacing a few seconds later with water sparkling on his red hair. "Okay, got a timer?"

"I'll count off seconds."

"Ready then?"

I nod, trying not to think about the depths of blackness swirling down for hundreds of feet below Ed. And below me.

"Start counting!" Ed calls out, before pulling his head under the water.

"One-one-thousand, two-one-thousand," I start to count, watching a ripple of wake as Ed swims closer to the boat. He flips some sort of underwater somersault, followed by a sideways spin, and then he's on his back, underwater, looking up at me and smiling, his face visible through a few inches of water.

"Twelve-one-thousand, thirteen-thousand," I'm counting, not really paying attention to the number I'm counting off, as he swirls in the water and dives deeper, so deep he starts to fade from sight while swimming toward the boat.

For an instant, I'm afraid he might be going to rock the boat or something unsettling, but then I see him through the glass panel, waving and smiling up at me.

I can't help smiling back. "Twenty-two-thousand, twenty-three-thousand," the thousands, you know, are to pace myself, to make each number approximately a full second. I wave and Ed swims back over to the other side. I look that direction, fully expecting him to stick his head up from the water and ask how he did.

"Thirty-three-thousand, thirty-four-thousand."

But he doesn't come up for air. He stays underwater, smiling and waving and occasionally letting a tiny bubble escape through his nose, but otherwise staying well below the surface. He swims back and forth under the boat, waving to me through the glass panel three more times.

"One-hundred-ninety-eight, one-hundred-ninety-nine," I keep counting, unsure whether I should be worried or suspicious. He hasn't got an oxygen tank under the boat or something, has he?

As I think I may have said before, few things surprise me. Perhaps it's because I carry a huge secret myself—of that fact that I'm a dragon, that I can fly and breathe fire—that I go through the world half expecting that most people have a secret. Maybe their secrets are about something not so unusual, such as secret dance skills or martial arts training, or surviving something that might have killed a weaker person. Not to diminish those accomplishments, but they're at least *human*.

But knowing, as I do, that not all who walk among us are strictly human, and being surrounded, as I am, with a family who most certainly is *not* merely human, there's a part of me that's not surprised that Ed doesn't surface for a full six minutes.

Or that even when he does, he's still not panting.

He looks up at me almost sheepishly, as though he's afraid he might have gone too far and frightened me. He climbs into the boat over the side, tipping it precariously so that I throw myself against the other edge, not so much to balance it, but at least to keep it from capsizing.

I study Ed awhile, watching the water roll in rivulets down his shoulders and drip from the hem of his kilt.

He can hold his breath a long time underwater. A crazy long time. Maybe even an *inhuman* long time.

So, theoretically at least, if someone wanted to search the Caspian Sea for whatever it was that attacked me, Ed would be an excellent candidate for the job. Unlike a diver with an air tank, he wouldn't have to worry about the death-bent attackers pulling out his mouthpiece, cutting off his air supply. In that respect, Ed could do for me something no one else could do. He could find the creatures that attacked me and finally put a face to my fear.

But—and this is such a huge exception I feel guilty for even considering it—if I were to fly Ed to the Caspian Sea on my back, he'd have to know I was a dragon. To even consider making the journey would require me to first break the cardinal rule of our existence, and let on to someone what I truly am.

But we know, or at least suspect, that someone at Nattertinny Castle is a dragon. And if the Sheehys are dragons, maybe Ed isn't completely human, either? Such a possibility might explain a lot.

"How long?" he asks when I've been silent for a while.

"Six minutes."

He makes a face. "I could have gone longer, but I was afeared ye might be worried."

"How long can you go?"

He shrugs. "Never pushed my own limits."

"How long have you stayed under?"

He meets my eyes. I can see him debating his answer. There is more, more he could say, more he could tell me. I know this look too well because I've felt it from the inside. Wanting to say something that would give away a clue to who you really are, wanting to scream a blast of fire just to let everyone who's ever underestimated you know there is more to you than they can see, and you're not someone to be casually dismissed.

And vying with that longing to be known, the simple reality that if we are to survive, we must keep our true selves hidden.

The world would destroy us if they knew who we are.

I reach for his hand. He doesn't flinch away as I lift his hand closer to my eyes. His fingers are cold from the lake, and still wet, their gnarled tips swollen like raisins from the water.

In so many ways, it's a human hand. But his joints are stiff, his fingers bent inward, his skin thick, calloused, hardened. His nails are nubby and malformed, like the toenails of some people's smallest toe, like the body didn't feel a real nail was necessary, and only bothered to sprout a bit of cuticle waste.

"I was born that way," Ed explains as I study his hand. I press my fingertips to his. They are large and dense, but as I press against them, they press back, an affirmation of contact, a yearning to be known.

"Ed?"

"My name's not *Ed*. It's *Eed*." He pronounces it with a long *E* so that it rhymes with *feed* and *seed*. "It's short for Edan." The name retains the long *E* in its full form.

"Is that a Gaelic word?" I don't know much Gaelic. I only knew Cruikshank meant knob-kneed because I met someone with the name back in the states. But like his last name, which identifies a true fact about him, I can't help thinking his first name might also yield a clue to his identity.

"'Tis."

"What's it mean?"

The look is back, gentled now, but still a battle. To speak or not to speak? To reveal or to hide?

Perhaps he knows I can find a Gaelic-English dictionary easily enough, because revelation wins.

"It means *fire*."

My heart is thumping crazy hard now, maybe even harder than it did when I first stepped in the boat. Okay, fire. No big deal, right? I mean, his hair is fiery red. Maybe he was named after his hair.

But he lives in dragon-fire castle, of all places. And my grandmother knew a dragon around here once.

And Ed said he had days in abundance.

51

I have to know. My throat has gone dry and I lick my lips, trying to summon moisture from somewhere, but there is none inside me. My voice is raspy as I ask, "Why *fire?*"

He meets my eyes for only a second more, before turning his head away with a shrug, shutting me out.

I've pushed too far, and I haven't asked any of the questions I came to have answered. I still don't know anything about sea monsters or the Sheehys.

But Ed surprises me by wrapping his fingers around mine (I have been holding his hand this whole time). He whispers, "Are ye afeared of sea monsters?"

"I am afraid," I clarify slowly, trying to identify just what it is I am scared of, and keeping in mind that climbing into this boat was nearly more than I could handle, "of being attacked by something I can't see and don't know how to fight. I'm afraid of the enemy I don't understand."

"Who is yer enemy?" Ed asks.

"I don't know."

"Why did they attack ye?"

I startle at his question, flinching at its sharpness as it strikes so close to home. I don't know what attacked me, but I can guess why. Whatever it was attacked me because I was a dragon. But I can't tell Ed that. I can't even speak right now, my throat has gone so dry.

"Ye know?" His voice is filled with wonder, maybe even awe. Somehow he's read the answer on my face. "Why?" He turns his hand over so that mine is on top, and now he's studying it like it's not the most normal-looking hand in the world. My skin is on the brownish side, and my nails are clean, trimmed longish but not polished.

"Last evenin'," Ed whispers, "when I was runnin' toward the bull, I thought I saw somethin' through the rain. Your hand didna look the same as it does now."

He saw me. I had started to change, and he saw me. Is this why he was willing to spend time with me today, even though, as the Sheehys attested, he doesn't interact with anyone? He saw me, and instead of being repelled, he drew closer.

Why?

I close my eyes. I should not do this. It goes against every rule, against my better judgment. And if my parents found out, I'd get a lecture up and down and forever.

But when I open my eyes, Ed is still watching me patiently, his hand holding mine.

So I look at the hands between us, drawing his gaze to our linked fingers. And then slowly, subtly, I let my talons grow.

Chapter Seven

I am careful not to hurt Ed as my nails lengthen and sharpen in his hands. Bright red color suffuses my fingertips, and the outlines of scales emerge. I halt the process and meet his eyes.

They're round with wonder, aglow with something I can't name, but it's a welcoming thing, so I push a little further, letting my fingers lengthen, the red color deepen, the scales on my fingers solidify. The rest of me is still human.

I don't know if all dragons can do this trick, changing one part of themselves but not others, changing slowly by gradients, but I grew up practicing in front of a mirror with my sisters, challenging each other with weird combinations—only horns and tails, for instance, or mostly dragon with a human face—so I'm good at it in ways my mother, who never changed into a dragon at all until she was nearly the age I am now, will probably never be.

Ed studies my hands until, self-conscious, I change them back into human hands. Then he smiles at me, grabs a tackle box from the back of the boat, opens it up, and pulls out a contact lens case and a bottle of solution. "Hold this, if ye don't mind."

He places the case in my hands, fumbles with the solution until he's filled both reservoirs, and then he plucks out his right contact, revealing an emerald eye which sparkles with such brightness it takes me a moment before I can look at it directly. He pulls out the other lens as well, and I'm staring into eyes that are green, vibrant, jewel-toned green, with just a bit of blue.

They are, quite possibly, the most beautiful thing I've ever seen.

Ed looks slightly sheepish, but hopeful.

I wet my fingertips with a bit of his contact lens solution, then reach up and pluck a lens from my own eye. I can see its ruby color reflected in Ed's eyes.

With no case to save it in, I slip the contact back into my eye.

"Yer a dragon?" Ed asks in a whisper, as though he might be overheard, even though we're alone in the lake, at least half a mile from the nearest person, though even the shore looks abandoned at the moment.

I nod, aware of what he's guessed. He knows I'm a *dragon*, even though I only showed him my hands and one eye. Without prior experience of dragons, no one would know that's what I am. They'd more likely guess demon or monster. "I can't show you anything else, not here. Anybody looking for the Loch Ness Monster might see me."

Ed glances around. There aren't any boats nearby, nor tourists with binoculars. An eager grin flashes on his face and he hands me his contact case, then dives back into the water.

"Yer not afeared of sea monsters?" he confirms again.

"Not unless they attack me."

"I promise not to attack. Yer safe with me." He ducks his head underwater and then swims in a wide circle in that void space below the surface, where the water is not yet too deep for me to see him. And as he swims, his body lengthens and changes. His arms with their funny, nubby hands, turn to a sort of flipper. His neck stretches thick and serpentine, his tail undulates behind him.

For an instant, I see the Loch Ness Monster as every witness has ever described it, save for the kilt, of course.

And then he shrinks back to Ed and grins up at me, no different than moments before when he'd shown off his ability to hold his breath.

He grabs the edge of the boat and pulls himself back in, grinning broadly.

"You're the Loch Ness Monster," I whisper, the volume of my voice lost to breathless wonderment. I'd known, or at least suspected, that Ed was something special.

But he's more than special.

He's legendary.

"Shh. Aye, that I am." He looks around to make sure he hasn't been seen. The lake is calm and silent. "Will ye take me, then?"

"To the Caspian Sea?" I feel humbled that he wants to go with me. That he revealed himself to me, after so many thousands of tourists have searched for him for so many years.

He nods solemnly. "I've never met another sea dragon."

"Sea dragon." I repeat the term he used. Not *monster*. That's only the name people have given him, because they were afraid of him, even though he was more afraid of them, of being found out or attacked or studied by them. It's a sad truth about the world we live in, and only reinforces why I conceal my identity. How very precious, then, that I can share who I am with Ed, and he with me. But I have to clarify. "You're the only one? The only sea dragon?"

He nods. "I've known a few dragons, the regular kind, with wings to fly. Have ye got those?"

"Yes."

"That's all there is. Dragons. Winged dragons that fly. No other sea dragons. I've researched all I can about myself. There are myths, of course. Ye might call me a hydra. That's what the sea dragons were called in the myths from long centuries ago."

"Hydra?"

Ed shrugs. "It means sea dragon. Some hydras had nine heads, or three, in the myths. But I've just got the one. Never met another kind, or another hydra at all."

I clasp his hand again. For all its strangeness, it's oddly familiar. Ed is more like me than anyone I've ever met, outside my own family. I want to hold this hand and not let go. At the same time, I hate to deliver disappointing news. Still, I'd rather he know now than find out later, after he's gotten his hopes up. "I don't think the creatures that attacked me in the Caspian Sea were hydras. They were smaller. And not so serpentine."

56

"Ach." Ed uses an exclamation, more clearing-of-the-throat than word, that I've heard other Scots use. It's a sort of acknowledgement, and in this case I take it to mean, *that may well be.* "I didna expect to have too much I common with any creature that would seek to harm ye. Nor did they sound from yer description like they'd be my own kind. But I've got to have a look, just the same. Ye ken?"

Ken. He's used that word a few times now. It's like the second half of *reckon*, to *think*. But more than that, to *understand*. Do I understand why Ed would want to travel all the way to the Caspian Sea and risk his life to find creatures that may or may not be like him?

"I ken." I ken on a level I can't even put into words, and I want to do everything I can to help him, whether that means carrying him on my back all the way there, or explaining to my mother why we won't be around for a few days.

"Shall we head back to the castle, then? Or did ye want to see more of the loch?"

"I've seen more of the loch than I'd hoped to see." I squeeze his hand before I let go.

For a second Ed looks at me, his green eyes welling with unspoken things, more than words could ever speak. Then he opens the contact lens case and slips the dusky disks over his eyes, hiding himself from the world again.

Maybe we should be making plans for our trip, or talking logistics, or something practical like that, but the whole way back to the castle, rowing the boat and then driving in the truck, all I can do is sit in silence and absorb what I've discovered.

Ed is the Loch Ness Monster. Excuse me, *Eed* is a hydra who happens to occasionally inhabit Loch Ness. I wonder how old he is. I wonder if he knew my grandmother, too, or if just the Sheehys did. I wonder if sea dragons are the same species as regular dragons. Probably not, right? I mean, Ed doesn't even have wings. It's not like he and I could ever have anything romantic between us.

He's safe. He's totally safe. I can be friends with him without any awkwardness, because we're not even the same species. I don't have to worry about developing feelings for him or ruining my plans to stay single forever.

But I don't say any of this aloud, some of it because can you imagine how awkward that conversation would be? But mostly because I'm still absorbing everything, and I need this silence, this undisturbed, sacred quiet, to come to terms with all I've discovered. More than that, I need to prepare myself for what's to come.

Because finding out Ed is a hydra is just one step toward my goal of learning what attacked me in the Caspian Sea. We've still got to get there, a journey of about 5,000 miles. And then Ed's going to go in the water. Into that deep, dangerous water.

And while he does that, I'm going to, what? Hover nearby? Go with him in the sea? The thought makes the blood chill in my veins. I mean, I nearly died down there. About the only thing more terrifying than going in the water, would be trying to float on top of it like when I was attacked from below.

But before we even have to worry about that, we have to talk to my mom. I'm not going to attempt to hide our trip from her because I'll have to be gone long enough she'd notice and worry. And besides that, she's made many journeys of some distance before and might have some tips for me. And there's also a part of me that feels like somehow, even from 5,000 miles away, I'll be safer if my mom knows where I am.

Ed rolls the truck to a stop at the gate and I hop out to open it. When I climb back in, he asks, "Want me to roast a cow for lunch?"

"The Sheehys won't mind?"

"I only ever eat me own cattle." He explains, making a thoughtful face as he guides the truck along the rutted track. "If I'd known what ye were last evenin', I'd have cut ye a bigger steak."

"It's okay. My appetite's usually only big when I'm a dragon. We flew to Scotland on a plane, not as dragons. My mom has this thing about going through customs and getting all our paperwork in order when we enter a new country for the first time."

"We'll take a plane to the Caspian Sea, no?"

Having just endured a transatlantic flight to get to Scotland, I make a face. "This will be a short trip. I'll use my wings, thank you."

"I canna fly." Ed reminds me, his tone apologetic.

"You can ride on my back."

"I'm heavy."

"It's okay. I used to fly around the village with my friends on my back all the time, even when I was a lot smaller than I am now. It's only really hard when you're taking off, especially if you have to climb. If I can catch a good tailwind you won't cause me any more trouble than flying into a headwind. Part of it has to do with aerodynamics, too. If you tuck in close to my neck where you won't cause much drag, I'll hardly know you're there."

"'Tis a long journey."

"Not quite five thousand miles as the crow flies. We'll have to take it in stages, but I should be able to make it in two nights."

"And during the day?"

"I know of a safe place where we can rest halfway there. I'll need my sleep then, for sure."

"And ye'll need yer strength up. I'll roast ye a cow for lunch." Ed parks the truck in a garage converted from the old stables. "Meet me in the courtyard in half an hour?"

"I'll see you then."

I hurry away to find my mother. She's probably going to be freaked out by my plans, not because she doesn't trust me, and not because I'm not perfectly capable of taking care of myself, but just because she's my mom and worrying about me is part of her job description, or something like that.

Fortunately she's not too hard to locate. She's in the sitting room of our suite, basking on a sofa in front of a cheery fire, reading one of the many novels that weighed down her suitcase. She's got her shoes off with her feet at the end of the sofa nearest the fire.

"Hey, Mom?"

She holds up one finger. This is her longstanding signal that she is aware someone wants her attention, but that unless the house is literally on fire or some other life-threatening emergency, she wants to get to the end of the paragraph she's reading before anyone interrupts her.

So I wait, planning what I'm going to say, until she lowers her finger and tucks her bookmark into place.

She smiles at me. "You and Ed have a good morning?"

"It's *Eed*." I correct her pronunciation. "We had a great morning. He's the Loch Ness Monster."

"Really?" She sits up a little straighter.

"Well, technically he's not a monster. That's just what people call him who don't know him. He's a hydra." I answer matter-of-factly, like I even know what a hydra is. "Anyway, since he's a sea dragon, and he's kind of an expert on sea monsters, he wants to go check out the Caspian Sea with me. You know, to learn about whatever it was that attacked me last summer." I try to keep my voice calm, like this is all completely normal. I don't want my mom to freak out. But my heart is running in terrified circles around my ribs, and she can probably hear that in my voice.

She sits up even straighter. "Is he also an expert on seaweed?"

"Mom, it wasn't seaweed, okay? This is precisely why Ed and I want to go check out the lake—because he wants to know what other sea monsters are out there, and I need to prove that I was attacked by something real."

My mom sighs. "Two things, Wren. One: if there's nothing there, then you're wasting your time and going for no reason. And two: if there *is* something there, if these creatures really did attack you, then they're dangerous. Why would you purposely go where it's dangerous?"

"So we're just supposed to avoid the Caspian Sea forever, now? If I find out what's down there, we'll know. We'll know for sure that it's dangerous and why, so we can learn how to protect ourselves."

Now my mom stands. She's not so much angry as pleading. "Dragons are almost extinct, Wren. My goal, my only purpose in life ever since I learned who I was and fell in love with your father, has been to do my part to keep dragons from going extinct."

"You had five kids, Mom. You've done your part."

"Only if those five kids find mates and have children of their own."

I stagger backwards a couple of steps. Didn't we just have a conversation last evening, in which my mom more or less said she understood that I was never going to find a mate and have kids? Or was she only agreeing that we should let my sisters have first dibs on the Sheehy brothers? "Mom, what are you saying?"

"I don't want you to get hurt. I don't understand why you think you need to go to the one spot on earth where you came closest to dying. I brought you into this world so you could live and have dragon babies of your own someday."

I breathe out a long breath and try to overlook everything she just said about dragon babies. I could say a lot of things on that subject, but none of them is going to get me any closer to the Caspian Sea. Instead, I focus on *my* goal, which is to figure out what attacked me so I can make sure I'm never, ever caught off guard, attacked, and nearly killed, ever again.

"Mom, we'll be careful. Ed saved me from the bull last night, remember? And Malcolm Sheehy said Ed's very safe, the best person on earth to take a person to Loch Ness. I think he's the best person on earth to keep me safe at the Caspian Sea, too. So unless we're all planning to avoid the Caspian Sea for the rest of our lives, I think I'll be safest if Ed finds out what's out there. If there's anything out there." I add in that last part out of deference to her seaweed theory, not because I believe it for a second, but because I know if I don't acknowledge it, she'll drag it into the conversation again.

Mom makes a face. It's one of her faces from right out of the mistakes-that-age-you articles, with her lips all pursed and pinchy, and her brow furrowed like one of those before-Botox pictures.

Just when I'm starting to think her face is going to freeze that way if she holds that expression any longer, she gives me one of those looks that says she'll consider giving her permission, on one condition.

I brace myself for what that condition might be.

Mom sets down her book and turns toward the door with an air of finality. "I need to talk to Ed first."

Chapter Eight

"Ed's in the courtyard roasting a cow," I inform my mother, then follow her there.

I can smell the roasting meat before we even step outside. As promised, Ed has an entire beef carcass roasting on the spit in the courtyard.

He turns and smiles as we enter. "Lunch'll be ready in just a few minutes."

"Ed?" My mom pronounces it correctly, with the long *e* sound. "I need to talk to you."

"Alright."

She glances back at me. "Alone."

"What?" I look around the courtyard. It's just me. What's she going to say to Ed that I'm not supposed to hear? "I'm just here for lunch. Don't mind me."

But Ed takes my mom through the wooden door in the curtain wall, leaving me alone with the roasting beef.

I stand there for a few minutes, waiting, listening, but I can't hear anything of what they're saying, and I'm pretty sure the meat is ready to eat. "I'm just going to help myself to lunch." I call out.

"Fine," Ed's voice carries back over the wall.

So I use Ed's sword and the pitchfork utensil to cut myself a heaping portion, though it's not as easy as Ed made it look last evening, and I sit down and eat, every minute expecting them to return through the door in the wall, but they're taking their time over there and don't return to the courtyard until I'm halfway through my second helping of steak.

"What did you guys talk about?" I ask when they finally return.

Ed looks chastened and doesn't answer.

"If we'd wanted you to know, we'd have included you in the conversation." Mom grabs a plate and waits for Ed to cut her some meat.

"Mom. Secrets?" I'm calling her out on breaking her own rule. My mom hates secrets on account of her dad didn't tell her she was a dragon until she was eighteen years old. Even though it was for her own protection, she was still offended that he kept something so important from her for so long, so now she has a policy against keeping secrets unless it's absolutely necessary.

But she carries her plate over to the table and sits beside me, shaking her head vigorously. "We just had a talk."

"Then why can't you tell me what it was about?"

"You'll know when you need to know, dear." She tears into her meat with the kind of total absorption that says our conversation is over.

Ed carries a plate over and sits opposite us, again at the far corner. But this time, I got smart and sat in the middle of the table. My mom is on the other side of me, furthest from Ed.

So maybe it's not so much that he doesn't want to sit by me, as that he's done talking to my mom, at least for now.

Respecting that, I eat in silence, consumed with chewing and swallowing (if I'm going to build my strength up for a long flight carrying someone as heavy as Ed, I need to eat). When I look over at Ed a few moments later, he's looking at me, a half smile on his lips even though he's chewing, and a gleam in his eyes I can see even through the dusky contacts.

When he sees me looking back at him, he smiles bigger.

I can't help smiling back. I mean, how many people can say they've eaten a steak dinner with the Loch Ness Monster? Even if he's not a monster.

*

The rest of the day is consumed with preparations. I study maps with my mom, making sure I know exactly where the safe resting spot is in Romania, a little over halfway to home. I don't have any swords with me on account of we flew here in an airplane, and can you imagine trying to get those past security? Even if we packed them in our checked luggage, it's not worth it to draw attention to ourselves.

But that means we'll only have Ed's broadsword and some knives with us for the journey. Normally, I know, most people don't worry about bringing swords and knives with them when they travel, not even through Romania, but we're not most people.

As I may have mentioned before, dragons are nearly extinct, and the reason for that is because we've been hunted down and killed so that we're almost all gone. Plenty of predators have contributed to our demise over the centuries, but our biggest enemy is currently a woman named Eudora, the very same person who lured my grandmother Faye to Siberia, which ultimately led to her death.

Eudora is not technically the one who killed my grandmother. She was behind her death, but the final blow was dealt by the yagi, which are these creepy soulless creatures Eudora created in a lab during World War Two. The yagi are a crossbreed between mercenary soldiers, and cockroaches. I know, I know, those two things don't seem remotely compatible, and normally they wouldn't be, but Eudora used dark magic to meld their DNA. The yagi are dragon hunters. They exist for one purpose: to hunt down and kill dragons.

The other thing about Eudora is, besides trying kill off all the dragons in the world, she's also furious at my mom, on account of my mom is the one who changed Eudora from being a dragon, to only human. Which you would think, given how much she hates dragons, would make Eudora happy, except that Eudora has always said the best weapon against a dragon is another dragon, and now that she's no longer a dragon, she's lost some of her skills, but none of her ruthlessness on her quest for dragon blood.

So the big thing about the trip will be staying out of sight, both out of human sight and away from the yagi. We'll fly at night, even though that's when the yagi are most active. We have no choice. If we flew in the daytime, we could be easily seen by anyone. Even at night, we have to keep our glow to a minimum, avoid flying over populated areas, and stay low enough to avoid radar detection.

And in case you're wondering, there's a zillion reasons why we don't want humans to see us. For one thing, humans don't realize we exist, so seeing us would freak them out and maybe, considering how many people carry phones with cameras and even video capability these days, cause a sensation and mass hysteria, besides giving Eudora a huge clue to our whereabouts.

But more than mass hysteria, which would be ugly but not necessarily fatal, we can't let the humans know we exist because traditionally, humans have been dragons' greatest enemies. They're afraid of us, so their first instinct is to kill us. Even if they let us live, they'd probably round us up and study us in a lab somewhere, or dissect us slowly to figure out what makes us different. And if they realized we had treasure hoards hidden away, they'd for sure confiscate those.

The only humans who are allowed to know who we are, are the members of the dragon world—the trusted few who love and support us, and rely on us for protection. That's how it worked for untold millennia, you know. Every village used to have their own dragon. The dragons kept the peace, watched over their people, and generally made life pleasant for human beings.

But then land-hungry, power-hungry, war-hungry people began to realize that to conquer their neighbors, all they had to do was defeat their dragons. The great conquerors recognized that killing dragons was hard work, but they discovered that if they could turn people against their own dragons, the people would all but defeat themselves, slaying their own dragons and thereby clearing the way for invaders to conquer them.

That's where all the bad stories about dragons started. You've probably heard them—myths that claim dragons are horrible, cattle-stealing, land-scorching, maiden-sacrificing beasts.

We're not. As far as I know, none of us have ever done any of those things. Even if it happened once or twice, it was always the exception, and probably for some good reason, like stealing a cow to feed a hungry village, or something.

But whatever. With rumors like that saturating human consciousness, we simply can't let ourselves be seen, so I'll be flying low, by night, with Ed on my back, all the way to Azerbaijan.

"You have to check in with your father before you go to the sea," my mom insists as we're uploading maps to my tablet (which I charged) so that I can check it if I need to, even if there's no Wi-Fi signal. "Ever since your attack, he's been looking into what you may have encountered in the sea."

This is news to me. "I thought you guys had written it off as seaweed."

My mom sighs. "I would like for it to just be seaweed. Wouldn't that be so much easier for everyone if it was something innocent, and not an unknown enemy hunting us from beneath the water?"

"Except that if it's not seaweed, we need to know so we can defend ourselves."

"That's why I'm letting you go, even though it scares me so much," my mom's voice hitches up a tiny, emotional notch. "You *will* talk to your father first, won't you?"

"Of course I will." Crap, she's not going to cry on me, is she? My mom likes to think of herself as this fierce dragon, and all, but she cries sometimes. And sometimes, when *she* cries, *I* cry.

I do *not* need that right now. I clear my throat. "What has Dad found out?"

"I don't know any details. You know we can't discuss these things over the phone." My mom and dad have this policy—which is probably prudent, all things considered—against saying anything over the phone that might give away that we're dragons, on account of someone (like maybe Eudora) could be listening in. "But his spies have reported Eudora's been visiting a Siberian lake for several years now."

"And you didn't say anything sooner?"

"We don't know why she's been visiting the lake. It could be anything."

"And it could be that she's making water yagi." I invent a term that's really not anything new, just the combination of two of my greatest fears—the yagi, and whatever attacked me in the water. But if Eudora is part of the equation, it makes sense. Too much sense.

"The spies haven't seen anything conclusive."

"How close have they gotten?"

"Not close enough to be seen."

"Hmm." I don't say anything more, because what else is there to say? If dad's spies don't get close enough to be seen, they're really not going to be able to see too many details, not even with binoculars. But I can't be too picky, because the spies aren't really high tech secret agents or anything, just villagers from our tiny mountain kingdom, who care enough about our welfare to make sure we know what Eudora's up to, even at the risk of their own lives.

If it hadn't been for our spies, my grandfather would never have known that Eudora had my grandmother Faye locked away in her lair. And my grandparents never would have met and neither my mother nor any of us kids would exist. Dragons would be even closer to being extinct than we are right now.

So I appreciate the spies. I just wish there was more they could tell us, on account of, you know, my life and maybe even Ed's life depends on what's under the surface of the sea, whether Eudora specifically bred it with black magic to kill us, and what abilities she may have given it for doing so.

"I think I have everything I need," I announce as I tuck my tablet into my backpack. Normally I'd wear the pack on my back, but with Ed riding there, it might get awkward, so he can wear it for me, along with whatever he's packed for himself.

"It's not yet night," Mom notes, her way of telling me I can't leave yet. "It won't be dark for another hour or two."

"But have you seen the low-lying cloud cover? I checked the weather radar. The clouds stretch to the North Sea. If I fly east from here, I'll be hidden by clouds, then over the water for a good stretch. By the time I reach the coast of the Netherlands or Germany or wherever I hit the mainland, it'll be plenty dark out. I've got to make it over halfway to get to our safe place in Romania."

My mom gives me that resigned look that says she'd argue with me if she could find any fault with my plan, but she can't, so she'll have to resign herself to watching me fly off toward danger even sooner than she'd expected. "Let's see if Ed's ready, then."

We find Ed in the courtyard roasting a brace of chickens. "I figured ye might be hungry, but a whole cow would be a heavy meal before flying. Chickens seemed right."

I can't help smiling at his thoughtfulness, and also because roast chicken sounds awesome. "Perfect. Then I'm ready to leave."

I eat a couple chickens, grateful that Ed is an accomplished cook. Fire roasting can be tricky, especially with something relatively small like a chicken. It's too easy to incinerate the bird completely, or end up with parts undercooked. But Ed's basted the birds on the spit while cooking them over a low fire, so the meat is juicy and tender.

When we're finished eating, Ed shows us the underwater camera equipment he's bringing. It looks like pretty high tech stuff, even if it is a few years old. In Ed years, that's nothing. I feel slightly better knowing we have a way to look at the monsters before we swim with them.

Then Ed carefully stows the equipment in his backpack along with his spare clothes and other supplies. He hoists the pack over his shoulder, along with the huge scabbard that holds his broadsword.

Ed leads me and my mom up the stairs that spiral through the tallest tower of the castle. "Ye mentioned taking off is the hard part, climbing in the air with a burden on yer back. Thought this might make it a touch easier on ye."

"It will help. Thank you." I review the plans with Ed, making sure he knows what to expect, since it's going to be almost impossible for us to talk once I'm in dragon form. Most dragons, when they're in dragon form, can't talk at all. Our forked tongues and the shape of our mouths when we're dragons make it really tricky to form words. Dragon mouths are made for breathing fire, not speaking words. They're more like beaks than lips. But my sisters and I used to practice talking as dragons, so I can make sounds that are sometimes recognizable as words. It's tricky, and far from optimum, but it works in a pinch.

Still, I prefer to work out all the kinks ahead of time.

When we're done discussing preparations, Mom asks, "You're sure you don't want to wait for your sisters to get back so you can tell them goodbye?"

"Who knows when that will be? I'm not going to interrupt their fun." I don't say it out loud, but I want my sisters to enjoy their time with the Sheehy brothers, even if they aren't dragons. They don't need to be distracted by my plans. "Anyway, I'll be back in a few days. Everything's going to be fine."

My mother nods solemnly. I can tell she's trying to keep it together, but she's scared for me. I give her a big hug. "We'll be fine, mom. I'm doing this to make the world a safer place for dragons. You understand?"

"Yes. I'm proud of you for facing your fears. I just wish…"

"Hmm?"

"I wish it wasn't so dangerous."

Rather than allowing myself to think about the danger, I turn to Ed. "You're all ready?"

"Aye."

Chapter Nine

I turn to my mother and peel off the fluffy white terrycloth robe I've been wearing, which I borrowed from my en suite bathroom. Underneath it, I've got on the clothes my mother designed for us girls to wear when we transform into dragons. See, we grow and change shape so dramatically that most clothes get ripped to shreds in the process, which isn't a huge deal, except that when we change back, we're naked, which is almost always awkward.

But considering that our dragon waists stay pretty tiny (though our dragon hips get enormous) my mom designed these pleated skirts with elastic waists that keep us covered when we're human but don't bust off or get in the way when we're dragons. Mine's a deep red color, to match my dragon scales.

The top part of our bodies is trickier to fit. We sprout wings from our shoulder blades, which is why backpacks stay on as long as the straps can adjust to accommodate our growth. Taking advantage of that, my mom created racer back tops made from really stretchy material, with adjustable straps that slide wider instead of snapping to bits when we grow. The only trick is, we have to slide them back to a short setting when we turn back to humans, but that's a far cry handier than being completely naked.

I turn back toward Ed. He's averting his eyes politely, but at the same time, he's fighting back a smile that says he got enough of a glimpse of me to realize he likes what he saw.

While this might make me feel self-conscious, I actually find it flattering, especially when you consider Ed's hundreds of years old and spends part of his time in a lake, where people actually go swimming, never mind that it's crazy cold. So I'm sure he's seen enough scantily-clad women over the years that it ought to take more than a little skin to impress him. And besides that, I've seen him several times now without his shirt on, and quite appreciated the view, so I suppose it's only fair.

But now is not the time to worry about any of that. I pull myself up, straightening, stretching, growing, taking care not to bump into Ed or my mother as my wings sprout widely and my body swells. When I turn to Ed in full dragon form, he's grinning with a smile he doesn't bother to hide.

I dip my head to look him in the eye, though my head is now far larger than his, and my eyes set more on the sides of my head than the front, which is great for getting a wide-angled view, spotting predators approaching from any direction, or scanning the horizon, but makes me look cross-eyed whenever I focus on anything straight in front of me.

Ed places one gnarled hand on the bridge of my dragon nose. "Yer beautiful," he says, with true awe and appreciation in his voice.

I've never once wondered whether I'm beautiful as a dragon. Very few people have ever seen me as such, anyway, and none have bothered to comment until now. But I feel a rush of warmth at Ed's words and the sincerity behind them. I'm horned, scaly, reptilian—pretty dang terrifying, by most measures.

And to Ed, I'm beautiful.

I crouch low and he climbs on my back. My mom, who's carried people on her back before, as well as ridden on my dad's shoulders before she learned how to change into a dragon herself, gives Ed some tips for holding on, staying close to minimize drag, and generally making it easier for me to haul him through the sky.

Then I clamber up onto a sturdy parapet and take off with a leap, wings outstretched.

Oh, wow.

Ed is heavy.

I know he mentioned that before and I dismissed his concerns, but the man is sincerely substantial. I happen to know, being a dragon myself, that even when we're in human form, we're unusually dense. It's like all those muscles and fibers that expand to make a dragon are compressed inside our human bodies.

And when you consider how big Ed is, even without the compression factor…well, he's heavy.

I feel the strain immediately, and have to beat my wings to reach the cloud cover above us before we fly past the Nattertinny Castle property line. For a few struggling moments I wonder if maybe this wasn't a crazy idea after all, or if I'm even up to the challenge. But then I catch an updraft and start to glide and fix my eyes resolutely on the trip before me. I can do this. We'll make it. We have to.

I'm tired of living in fear.

*

Ten hours later, as dawn is breaking over Romania and I'm still not to the safe resting place, I realize I am, indeed, completely crazy. I had some friends who ran a marathon during college last year, and they limped around sore and weak for days afterward. In a lot of ways that's what I've just done, only I've got to do it all again tomorrow, and without a couple of hours of flying through clouds before the sun goes down to give me a head start.

Granted, I will be a little over halfway home once I make it to our safe place, but I had a good tailwind most of the way today, which helped. I don't know what kind of wind I'll get tomorrow.

Finally, just as the sun is starting to come up in earnest, I spot the familiar abandoned castle where I've stayed with my family on trips before. My parents discovered it years ago while fleeing the yagi, and they've since done some research into the place. It's one of those unfortunate estates that were seized by the government after the First World War, which were supposed to be returned to their rightful families in the decades since the country became a republic. But no descendants of the original family have ever stepped forward to claim it, and so it sits in limbo, belonging essentially to no one. Given its remote location in the mountains, with no paved roads leading anywhere near it and any previous paths overgrown by time, hardly anyone on earth seems to realize it exists.

So we don't feel guilty using it as an overnight resting spot. We've even patched up some of the broken windows and closed doors to help preserve the place from the elements, should the rightful heirs ever decide they're up to the challenge of restoring the mammoth structure.

Not that any of that matters now. My toes are slapping against the topmost branches of trees as I lose the updraft in preparation for landing. I stumble forward on weak legs as I set down in the woods near the castle. Exhausted, I don't wait for Ed to climb off my back before I shrink back to my human form.

Ed's arms are still around my shoulders, and he props me up, adjusting my top for me as I sag against him. My right eye socket is smooshed against his left collarbone, but I'm too exhausted to care. Also, he smells good, like the open sky and something distinctively Ed which I've decided I rather like.

"What can I do fer ye?" he asks.

"Water," I rasp, thirsty from my long flight.

Ed's got a water bottle clipped to a belt loop on his kilt, and he opens it and holds it to my lips, tipping it just enough so I can drink, a few weak swallows at a time, without choking in my weariness.

"Are we stayin' the night in that castle?"

"Yes. There's a secret entrance, but we need to eat first." I speak slowly, too tired to talk at full volume. I'm not even sure if Ed can hear me, the way my face is buried against his chest, but I don't have the strength to support myself. It's all I can do to stay awake.

"Want me to hunt something?"

"That would be great."

Ed spends the next couple of minutes making sure I'll be okay without him there to prop me up. He makes a sort of pillowed resting spot with our backpacks propped against some big rocks, and I sag against them, welcoming the oblivion of sleep until he nudges me awake to announce he has roasted meat.

My hunger is even stronger than my exhaustion, and I tear into the meal with trembling hands. Ed helps me, bestowing me with venison in small portions, practically hand-feeding me, which normally I wouldn't tolerate but under the circumstances is a welcome relief. I'm falling asleep by the time we finish the meal.

"I hate to wake ye," Ed apologizes, "but don't we need to go inside?"

He's right. We may be in a remote area, but outside the safety of the castle walls, we'd be easy prey for the yagi, especially asleep. "Can you help me stand?"

"I can do one better." He scoops me up, cradling me in his arms. For an instant I'm caught off guard, but then I realize I'd probably be more of a burden to him if I insist on walking, and I'd only slow us down. Besides, I think I like being in his arms. So comfy.

From here I can see the rock formation that hides the secret back entrance to the abandoned castle, and I point Ed in that direction. In spite of his size and the two backpacks hanging off his back, he's able to carry me through the tunneled entrance without bumping me into anything. My brothers discovered the entrance while they were exploring the place once when we were staying here as kids. Before that, we only ever knew to fly in to the courtyard from above. All the other entrances are blocked off.

And even this route of entry, once we make our way through, we lock securely behind us by dropping a heavy iron beam into a catch plate, sealing off the inner door so no one can follow us in. We'll leave it open behind us when we leave so we can use that entry again on another visit.

"There's a well," I explain as we pass through the courtyard. "The water is good."

Ed stops and draws a bucketful, and I drink, every bit as thirsty as I was hungry. Then I point the way to a room I know of, with a small couch where my parents once spent the night. There are rooms on the second floor that still have beds in them, but the stairs seem impossibly far away, and this little room is so close.

Ed lowers me onto the loveseat and then acts like he's going to leave.

"Where are you going?"

"To find a room for me."

"Stay here. Keep me safe." To my relief, he doesn't take much convincing, but slumps besides me and puts his feet up on the marble-topped coffee table in front of us.

I flop onto his shoulder. The castle is chilly and I'm glad for his warmth.

*

I awake to bright sunlight and realize from the angle of the sun that it's late afternoon. I've slept most of the day, and I'm hungry. I'm pretty sure Ed has been asleep this whole time, but when I lift my head, he changes position, his green eyes opening sleepily.

"Ye hungry?"

"Famished."

"I'll go find us a meal." He eases out from under me and slips away.

For a moment, I consider trying to get up, but then decide it's not worth the effort. I tip over, resting my head on the empty section of the sofa that's still warm from Ed's body. I curl my legs up next to my chest and close my eyes again.

Before long Ed is back, awakening me to the promise of food, and I sit up to eat, marveling that Ed is so handy with hunting. It's something I'd always taken for granted before, because my dad always hunted and taught us to hunt. We dragons need a lot of calories to keep going.

While every member of my family understands the importance of hunting and eating meat, I've never met anyone else who places the same priority on consuming large quantities of meat, let alone possesses the skills to hunt and roast their prey.

Which raises another question I hadn't much thought about. Between bites, I ask Ed, "Can you breathe fire?"

"Aye. That's how I cooked yer food."

I accept his explanation, even though it seems at odds with what he is. Why would a sea creature need to know how to breathe fire? But I'm more interested in eating than talking, and I don't suppose that's a question Ed can really answer, any more than I could tell you why my wings are fireproof and my scales armored.

It's just how we are.

And anyway, there's another question that's been bothering me, burning inside me all through my flight last night.

"What did my mom want to talk to you about?"

"Lots of things." Ed's answer is noncommittal.

"Like what things?"

"She's worried for yer safety. She asked me questions about myself."

"Why couldn't she have done that in front of me?"

Ed looks me full in the face with his bright green eyes. Neither of us have bothered with contacts for this trip, because no one is supposed to see us anyway, and contacts are a bother. We packed them, but we're not wearing them. Ed shrugs off my question. "I dunno." Then he quickly raises another subject. "I don't think we should fly tonight."

"Why not?" I'm aware that he switched topics on me, but this new choice is a good one, and I wasn't getting anywhere with my line of questioning, so I let him switch. But I still wonder what my mom said to him, just the same.

"It's too far. Last night's journey was hard on ye. I don't want to wear ye out completely. Besides, it's been a year since ye were attacked. One more day won't make any difference. We're safe here. We should rest."

I mull his words. It goes against our plan, yes, but all his points are valid. I've never been so exhausted. The sun will be setting in a matter of hours. I won't have my strength up by then. "I'm not as strong as I thought I was," I admit softly, disappointed in myself.

"I'm heavier than ye expected," Ed says. "I was impressed ye made it as far as ye did. Ye just need your rest. Yer strong. Mighty strong." The last of his words are spoken in a soothing tone.

I've finished off whatever of the meat I'm going to eat, and now I sag back on the sofa, my eyes drooping downward, more relieved than disappointed that we won't be leaving tonight.

*

By the next afternoon, I'm starting to feel revived. Maybe not fly-another-two-thousand-miles sort of revived, but I can at least make it through a meal without falling asleep.

Ed is still concerned about our plans. I think part of his apprehension stems from a feeling of guilt that I've been carrying him. But he's also focused on making sure I don't overdo it. And maybe there's something to that.

So I listen, open-minded, as he presents a possible plan.

"If ye can fly us to the Black Sea and put down in the water, we can switch places. I can swim with ye on my back. I'm a very fast swimmer."

I can't argue with that. I'd read up on the Loch Ness Monster in preparation for our vacation, so I'm familiar with the accounts of the speed at which the monster was said to swim—faster than the cars on the road, faster than boats with motors. And I was planning on flying across the Black Sea anyway. Ed's plan won't take us out of our way. In so many ways, his idea is brilliant, a perfect solution to the impediments that have stalled our progress. It would give me a chance to rest a bit, and even allow us an opportunity to travel by day, since we'll be not nearly so visible in the vast sea as we'd be up in the wide open sky.

There's just one problem.

"I'm afraid of deep water."

Ed's hand closes over mine, the look in his green eyes assuring me that he knows—that he's thought of that, he remembers my trouble on Loch Ness, whose cold waters aren't nearly as reminiscent of the Caspian Sea as its neighboring Black Sea will be. "I promise I'll keep ye safe. Can ye trust me?"

Chapter Ten

Ed's crazy. He's a crazy old monster on a lunatic mission to save me from my own irrational fears.

And as my mother could probably attest, I am just insane enough to go along with him.

"It would save us a lot of time, and allow us to travel by day." I acknowledge, not mentioning I'm reluctant to attempt another marathon flight so soon after the last one. The reasons I mentioned are enough on their own.

"It gives me a chance to share the work a bit, too." Ed looks at me with pleading in his eyes, and I realize this is about more than just getting to the Caspian Sea in the next day or two. As he'd mentioned before, there's no real hurry. If there's something down there, we're as likely to find it a week from now as we are tomorrow.

But there's more at stake here, isn't there?

From the beginning, Ed's mission has been two-fold: partly for him, and partly for me. For him, he wants to see these other sea creatures and learn if they're anything like him. He's been alone in this world for centuries. Being an oddball myself, I understand his desire to investigate.

But for me, he wants to find what attacked me so I don't have to fear it any longer. Part of that goal—maybe a large part, I realize now—is about helping me to not be afraid anymore, regardless of what's under the surface. Getting over that fear means going back in the water.

And this proposal is part of his plan to help me with that.

He's still got hold of my hand, and I link my supple fingers through his gnarled digits. "Ed?" I give his hand a squeeze.

"Aye?"

"Remember how scared I was to get into the boat on Loch Ness?"

"Aye. But ye did it anyhow."

"I'm going to be that scared again. Maybe even more scared. I might hold tight to your arm again, like I did before."

"I can handle yer fear." He grins suddenly, out of nowhere, in spite of the seriousness of our conversation. "I rather like it when ye hold tight to me."

Blame it on the fact that I'm still a little groggy from sleep, but for the next little who-knows-how-long, I just sit there looking at Ed and thinking about how lovely his eyes are without the dusky contacts, and how nice he's been to me, and what a pity it is he's been all alone in the Scottish Highlands for so many centuries.

But after however many minutes of eye-gazing, something turns over among my jumbled thoughts and sticks out above the rest, demanding to be acknowledged. I've pushed this thought away before.

Ed can breathe fire.

The fact taunts me a bit longer while I consider its significance.

Ed is a hydra, a *sea* dragon.

But he can breathe fire.

I have assumed, from the moment I learned Ed is capable of changing into a scaled reptile, that the reptile he can change into is distinctly different from the kind of reptile I am. And because of that assumption, I've reached the very safe conclusion that there can't be anything romantic between us.

But the way he's grinning at me now, and the way I'm gazing back with my heart feeling light and hopeful in spite of the danger that awaits us, I realize that assumption has led me to become far more familiar with him than I would have otherwise.

That's not a problem...so long as Ed's a sea dragon, and I'm a regular old dragon, and those are two completely different things, the end.

But it occurs to me, in a dreadful sinking-feeling sort of way, like maybe I've gotten into far deeper water than I'd realized, that maybe Ed and I aren't so different.

No sooner have I realized that, then I make up my mind, quite firmly, that I don't want to know. We still have a long road ahead of us and I need to cling to Ed, and I can't imagine doing that if he and I—

Nope.

Not going to think about it.

"Okay." I agree, perhaps a little too breathlessly, as though I've just fought a battle which I'm still not sure I've won. "Let's plan on that, then. Tonight I'll fly us to the Black Sea. And when we get there, I'll land on the water. You'll turn into a hydra and I'll turn back into a human, and you can take me to shore. We can fly tonight, float tomorrow, and then fly that last little bit the next night. That puts us two days behind schedule, but I won't have to fly so hard or so fast, so I won't sap my strength, or anything." Which seems prudent since there's every likelihood I might have to fight these water yagi creatures, if they do exist, which I believe they do. But I don't mention that, either.

That much decided, I stand, partly because I've been sitting so much for the past day-and-a-half, so standing feels good for a change.

And partly because I've been spending a lot of time close to Ed, and it occurs to me that maybe I need to put a little space between us. This will be my only chance for a while, since we'll be clinging to one another for the next day and a half.

"All right, then. Sounds good." Ed agrees. He stands as well. I half expect him to question whether I've made up my mind too quickly, or if I know what I'm getting into, but he doesn't. Instead he carries the bones from our meal out of the room.

I watch him go. He sounded as relieved to be done with the conversation as I felt.

Maybe these feelings between us are new and scary for him, too.

*

82

I'm no sooner in the air that night than I realize it's a good thing Ed and I already made plans to land on the Black Sea, because the wind is against me, pushing me back, and I have to fight it hard to make any progress. It takes me several hours to complete the trip across Romania, and then to reach a point far enough out to sea that we won't be seen by anyone on shore.

By then I'm feeling weak and trembly, even though the night is only half gone.

Fortunately I'm not as completely exhausted as I was when we landed two days ago. For one thing, I think that journey made me stronger, at least once I'd finally rested up from it. And for another, I simply haven't been flying for as many non-stop hours as I did that night.

So though I'm weak and winded, I still have the strength to float on my back on my dragon-wings, so reminiscent of that night when I was attacked. I keep my tail up out of the water, telling myself repeatedly that this is the Black Sea, not the Caspian Sea. Ed is with me and will keep me safe, no matter what.

Perhaps it's because I'm too tired to be terrified, or maybe it's because I've stuck close to Ed in spite of my fear of my growing feelings, which has somehow made me stronger in the battle against my fears. Or maybe simply being near Ed is a comfort. I don't know.

Whatever the reason, I manage to float on my back long enough for Ed to hand over the backpacks and his broadsword before he changes into a hydra.

I've only seen him in this form once before, and then only for a few seconds. And to be perfectly honest, I was so surprised by what he'd become that I didn't pay much attention to the details.

But I realize now, as he floats in front of me all green and glowing in the darkness, that he is beautiful, too. It's weird to think of him in those terms, because in human form he's sort of misshapen and wild. But he is a beautiful sea serpent, or hydra, or whatever.

By this point I'm at my limit of floating without freaking out, so I clamber onto his back while still in dragon form, and I situate the backpacks on my back and secure Ed's broadsword with the scabbard strap crossways over my chest so it won't fall off, because if I lose hold of it in the Black Sea it's going to sink like a rock and I am personally *not* going down after it.

And then I turn into a human being, which is a huge relief, and I slump across Ed's shoulders and hold on as he starts to move through the water.

At first, he doesn't go very fast, maybe because he's worried about my ability to hold on. Or possibly he's trying to find some fish to catch, because after a while he dips his head down into the water and flings a brown trout back my way, which is particularly thoughtful of him because not only was I hungry, but trout are one of my most favorite kinds of fish. And if you're familiar with the variety of fish that live in the Black Sea—sturgeons and scorpionfish and dogfish and lampreys—then you know he could have easily flung me a creepy breakfast instead.

So I cling to him with one arm and eat the fish with the other, and I don't feel guilty about it because Ed catches some fish for himself, as well. And when I'm done with that fish he catches me two more, and then I sag against his neck to rest, and he swims a little faster, but not so fast that I lose my hug-like grasp around his shoulders.

Morning dawns while I'm holding on, mostly oblivious and resting, and the sun rises and we're splashing and wet like a water ride at an amusement park, and I'm almost having enough fun to forget that I'm scared.

In fact, I'm trying to talk myself out of my fear as I cling there. I mean, I really don't have anything to be afraid of, certainly not here in the Black Sea, where I'm not even technically in the water except for my feet mostly, and the dips of the undulating motion Ed makes as he jets through the water, which sinks me in spray past my knees, dousing me sometimes up to my face if we hit a high wave just right.

Besides which, I need to learn to come to terms with this fear and move past it before we get to the Caspian Sea.

So I'm thinking these things, and breathing evenly, telling myself to enjoy this crazy ride, when I feel a tremor quake through Ed's body.

The first tremor is like a startle, a sort of what-was-that kind of jolt. The second tremor is bigger, a more sincere kind of fear, accompanied by a rearing up in the water that prompts me to wrap my arms and legs more tightly around Ed's shoulders.

And then I feel it, too—the reason for the tremors.

Something touched my leg. Something grasping, like a hand.

It was a brief instant of contact, and I'm not going to lie, it brought back a deluge of memories from last summer which I'm sure are influencing my perception of what's happening now, but what does that matter, really, in the face of the unrelenting truth?

That was *not* seaweed.

Ed picks up his speed and I bury my face against his neck, wincing and even kicking as mysterious underwater beings grasp my ankles, threatening to pull me off Ed's back. We jet through the water, faster, faster, so fast I'm sure we've got to leave whatever-it-is behind.

And then Ed rears up high and I look down into the blue-black waters of this enormous sea, and I see what I couldn't see that night when I was attacked and the glare of the sun seared the water.

Heads.

The same domed heads I only felt before as I wrestled with them in the water.

For an instant panic grips me and I want to scream, but Ed, perhaps realizing that he can't outrun them after all, whips about a quarter turn, striking the water with his spiked tail, knocking two heads together, dousing the sea with a cloud of red.

He swims on, faster again, whipping around once more and striking with his tail, so whatever it is under the surface gives an inhuman cry and rises partway above the surface, and I get the clearest glimpse I've had yet of this enemy that haunts my nightmares.

It's a human form, plus a couple sets of arms. A stiff, shiny, semi-human form. The creature attacking us is part human, part cockroach, part…fish? Shark? Squid? Eel? Or maybe an alligator or some type of crustacean, given the exoskeleton.

I don't know. I can only guess Eudora's black magic was behind this bastard spawn of mad science.

While it might be helpful to know what the beasts were bred from in order to best fight them, right now my biggest concern is getting rid of them, or getting away from them, at least. After all, I'm in human form right now. These things (they've got to be the same type of foe that attacked me last summer) nearly killed me when I was a dragon. I'm infinitely more vulnerable as a human.

But it's broad daylight out. I can't risk being seen.

I glance around the lake, trying to determine how much of a risk I'd be taking if I switch into dragon form.

Keep in mind, the Black Sea is huge. Its surface area is slightly larger than the entire state of California (I did a report on the Black Sea once for school in case you're wondering how I know this), so even though it's host to some pretty massive shipping vessels, they're few and far between given the size of the sea.

Not that I dare disregard their presence—the higher I fly, the more visible I'd be, no matter how far away the ship. And since I'm bright red as a dragon, I'd be vastly easier to spot than Ed's almost-sea-colored scales. But to my relief, I can't see any boats from where we are right now.

So in spite of those risks, I waste no more time in turning into a dragon and rising up off Ed's back, mostly because I cannot stand being so close to the nasty beasties a second longer. Everything inside me is screaming *get away!*

But also for two rational reasons. One: I need to escape from the sea beasties before they pull me under. And two: Ed's going to have a much better shot at effectively fighting them if he doesn't have to worry about me on his back.

Ed looks up at me and winks, then dives under the water.

I'm immediately concerned for his safety, never mind that he's a big bad sea dragon who can hold his breath infinitely longer than I can hold mine. I'm also worried about my own ability to keep him in my sight.

Granted, he glows. He's glowing brightly now, probably for my benefit (we dragons do have some control over how brightly we glow—but it's more emotional than physical. It's complicated. I can only assume sea dragons operate on a similar principle), but he's also swimming crazy fast, and I have to fly at a good clip just to keep up.

At the same time, I'm keeping an eye out for boats and planes and anything else that might have humans aboard who might see me or worse yet take my picture.

But even those two worries, crucial though they may be, are quickly eclipsed by a third concern.

Ed is massively outnumbered.

Never mind that he's considerably bigger than the swarming sea yagi. Their sheer quantity is overwhelming. Taken together, they've got to outweigh him, possibly multiple times over. Given that we don't know what they are, how they fight, or what they're capable of, (regular yagi have venom in their spurs—poison venom that once killed my parents' beloved dog. Who knows what these beasties might have?) it's fair to say my worst nightmare is coming true, but with a horrid twist.

They're not just after me.

They're bent on killing Ed, too.

Chapter Eleven

I've got to do something.

I can't just fly up here, watching these creatures swarm over Ed. He's whipping about with his tail and trying to use his horns, but that's about all he's got. It's pretty hard to breathe fire underwater, and he doesn't have regular arms like I do, with talons on my fingers. He's just got those flippers, which are super great at moving him through the water quickly, but otherwise useless against his enemies.

The yagi seem intent on pulling him down, and his glow has disappeared from my sight several times now as they dogpile him, forcing him deeper, too deep for me to see his green glow.

Furious at the mongrel monsters, I dive toward the water. I don't dare whip at the mass of yagi with my spiked tail, because Ed is down there, writhing among them as he tries to fight them off. I can't risk hurting him.

Nor am I keen on getting in over my head among them. They pulled me down too easily before, and there weren't nearly so many of them then.

That leaves me with little choice.

I fly at them swiftly, executing a practiced dip, skimming the surface of the water, reaching down just as I pass by the swarm, and plucking up a couple of monsters, flinging them high into the air.

In a blink, as they're airborne, tumbling through the empty blue sky with such furious multi-arm-flailing futility it's almost comical, I draw Ed's broadsword and swing it at the vulnerable seam between their heads and their bodies.

I've been trained to defend myself against regular yagi, which have an exoskeleton that's bulletproof. There are few effective ways to kill them. Our preferred method is to use a sharp blade to slice through the tiny seam between their bodies and their heads (they have no neck, creepy buggers).

And as I learn immediately, to my satisfaction and relief, these water yagi are much the same. I miss the mark on the first beast, the blade of the unfamiliar sword deflected by the yagi's armor. But I'm a quick learner and I hit my target on the second monster. A startled head flies free of the body with a pitiful squeal of dismay, tumbling back into the Black Sea. Its many arms stream behind, twitching lifelessly as land yagi do when they're beheaded, and then steaming as its soulless shell evaporates.

One down, untold masses of dozens to go.

Holding tight to the sword with my right hand (I can't risk losing it now), I skim and dip again, plucking up a water yagi with my left hand, flinging it high, swinging the sword as the beast falls down, taking two hacks to find the tiny crevice, severing its head from its body.

Now that I know how to kill them, I just have to repeat the process several dozen more times until they're all gone.

Preferably without losing sight of Ed.

Certainly before they overwhelm him or seriously injure him.

All without being seen, in spite of the fact that I'm a glowing, bright-red dragon flying through the clear blue sky.

I pluck up another, and as I'm swinging the sword at its neck, I try to count just how many sets of arms the creatures have.

One-two-three-four-five—

It sinks too quickly beneath the surface for me to be sure, the arms flailing so rapidly I may well have counted the same limbs over twice, and others not at all.

I pluck up another water yagi, tossing it extra high with a bit of spin, forcing the arms away from the body like a twirling hand-tipped skirt. I count both before and after I remove the head, starting at the face side so I don't recount the same arms twice.

One-two-three-four-five-six.

Six. Plus feet.

Eudora's bred them to an octopus, hasn't she? That explains why I felt so many sets of grasping hands in the Caspian Sea. But they still have the exoskeleton, the fish-like, shark-like features. How many kinds of DNA did she meld to make these creatures? They're even less human than the land yagi. Less human, more terrifying.

Determined to get the best of my enemies quickly, I set to work, dipping, flinging, hacking, killing. Soon I can smell that distinctive yagi stink rising up from the oily remnants of the carcasses in the water.

Yagi aren't natural creatures. They're bred in a lab (at least the land kind are—if they ever learn to breed in the wild we'll be done for), more black magic than science, and once they're dead, the magic that made them dissolves, and they quickly dissipate to nothing, save for the stink and the scum that's the residue of their evil selves.

As I repeat the steps that destroy my enemy, fueled by the fear of injury to Ed, I realize a couple of things. For one, I'm making progress. The swarm is slightly smaller now, replaced by a putrid scent in the sky. Maybe I'll get the best of these fiends…eventually. But this realization is countered by the second.

Killing yagi is hard work.

Being a dragon is exhausting (our metabolic rate jumps exponentially when we convert to dragon form), especially being a dragon after having just been a dragon flying into a headwind with a heavy hydra Scotsman on my back. But being a dragon and flying while fighting, swinging Ed's absurdly heavy broadsword, is more exhausting still.

So it's a battle, not just to kill the yagi before they kill Ed, but to kill them all before I'm so dead from exhaustion that I fall into the sea, unable to fight them off any more.

Dip.

Fling.

Hack.

Repeat.

Dip.

90

Fling.

Hack.

I can't begin to count how many times I've gone through the motions. The yagi are heavy. My arms are tired, and I can't throw them nearly as high anymore. Nor is my trembling sword arm as accurate as I'd like. Sometimes I beat them about with the sword like a piñata as they fall, and I don't even get their heads cut off before they hit the water. In fact, my ineffective attempts are starting to outnumber my successful beheadings.

Through groggy eyes I look down at the water. My intention is to gauge how many yagi remain. But when I look down, I see something that terrifies me far more than the largest swarm of yagi ever could.

Ed is gone.

Where did he go? He was right there the last time I looked, which couldn't have been that long ago. Granted, I'm disoriented from exhaustion, but there's really nowhere for him to go, save for the body of water larger than the state of California, which is over two thousand feet deep in places.

This is precisely why I didn't want to lose him—because finding him again might be impossible. Just think how many people have been looking for the Loch Ness Monster over the course of so many decades. They've yet to find him, even though that lake is thousands of times smaller than this one. If I lose him here, especially if he's injured or needs my help…

No. I can't lose him.

Concerned, I circle closer, flying lower over the water, aware that he may be traveling forward, away from me, even as I look for him in the vicinity of where I last saw him. But I can still see yagi below me. They're not so much at the surface now as they are roiling beneath it, but they're still there.

I never thought I'd be glad to see yagi, but as long as I can still catch a glimpse of them, I've got a decent idea of where Ed might be.

Just to be sure, though, I circle around low, hoping to spot a glimmer of glowing green beneath the surface.

Nothing.

Maybe then too, I should make note of where I am…just in case I don't find him for a very long time and have to find my way back to this spot. It's easy to get disoriented among the endless waves, each of which look the same as the last.

I survey the area. Sea. Sea. Sea. Fortunately I don't see any boats, save for a large shipping vessel that's little more than a speck in the distance to the north of me. Given how many times larger than me it probably is, and taking into consideration that we dragons have distance vision far superior to humans, I'm probably out of their sighting range.

To the south, though, I can see the faint dark line of the Turkish mainland. This doesn't completely surprise me, since our intended route was to take us on a somewhat southerly course across the lake, a direct line from Romania to Azerbaijan, which is east but also a bit south of the Black Sea. Besides that, the coastline curves north for a large portion of the middle of the sea, which is probably pretty much where we are.

While it's possible someone on land could be looking out to sea with binoculars or a zoom-lens camera, nonetheless, I'm more relieved than worried. The northerly bulge of coastline tends to be one of the more sparsely-populated parts of Turkey, save for the city of Zonguldak. But I don't see a city and I'm assuming we're further east than that by now. So I'm a tiny bit relieved, because the coastline gives me a landmark of sorts, and it also promises solid ground to rest upon, assuming I can muster the strength to glide there.

But that's the full extent of my relief, because Ed has been missing for long minutes now. I mean, I know he can hold his breath for longer than that under perfect conditions, but he's been fighting the water yagi, which probably ups his oxygen needs.

Where is he? What's he doing? Is he okay?

He's got to be tired. Maybe not quite as tired as I am, but still, pretty much exhausted.

Unsure what to do next, I slip the heavy sword back in the scabbard that's crossways across my chest. I fly lower, closer to the sea, where I'm less likely to be spotted by anyone on the coast or the shipping vessel. And I scan the sea for any sign of glimmering green or even sea yagi, which have disappeared completely, save for a few distant underwater shadows that may or may not be the creatures I've been killing, nor do I want to dive underwater to find out.

So now I'm starting to feel a little panicked. Where is Ed? What if I've lost him? He came here to help me, but all I did was lead him to an enemy he neither understands nor is equipped to fight.

I am a bad friend. Ed is the first dragon of any sort I've ever met outside of my own family, and the very first thing I've done is drag him off to the enemy.

I suck.

I am a horrible person. I'm a horrible dragon.

Maybe I *should* dive underwater and go look for him.

But if I do that, I'll be easy prey for the water yagi, exhausted and outnumbered as I am, and no one will ever know what happened to either of us. They won't even know where to look for us because we were so behind schedule already and should have reached Azerbaijan by now.

But if I don't go underwater, I may never see Ed again.

I may never see Ed again anyway.

So I'm circling, searching for any sign of Ed and wondering what to do, when suddenly something shoots out of the water far to the east of me.

I fly toward it like a shot, in time to see Ed, in full sea-dragon form, breaching into the air kind of like a whale, only much higher, so maybe more like a dolphin, only of course he's bigger than a dolphin and glowing green and I have never been so relieved to see anyone in my entire life because I was sincerely starting to think he was dead or lost forever.

I zip through the air toward him, studying him as well as I can from this distance to see if he's injured. A dragon's scales are pretty much bulletproof, save for our underbellies which are slightly softer and can be punctured by another dragon's horns or talons. But just because regular dragons are that way, doesn't mean Ed is equally impervious. I've still never nailed down how he's the same as I am and how he's different, mostly because I'm nervous about what I might learn and its implications for our friendship.

But this is a life-or-death question that's bigger than friendship, so it's a conversation we should probably have before too long.

He doesn't look injured, but he does have a distinctly panicked look on his face, like maybe he was getting as worried down there as I was feeling up here.

This is not encouraging.

Okay, so remember how I said before that my mom is really bad at keeping secrets? That's largely because we dragons tend to have pretty expressive faces. We're able to communicate nonverbally with just a look, which is helpful because when we're in dragon form, we pretty much can't talk at all.

So right now, as Ed is breaching through the air and I'm flying toward him, he gives me this look which shouts *get me out of here!*

Which makes plenty of sense considering I can see the swarm of yagi surfacing beneath him, and I would want out of there if I was there.

I fly toward him as fast as I can.

But then he splashes back down into the water and the yagi pounce on him and I don't know what to do. I mean, if he was in human form I'd fly over there and pick him up, but he's a freaking hydra right now, so in addition to being nearly as big around as I am and considerably longer, he's got to weigh, I don't know, more than I could probably carry on a good day. Enough to drag me down into the depths after him in my current state.

94

Not that I wouldn't be willing to risk that for his sake, but it's just that it wouldn't do either of us any good at all if I did.

I fly really, really close. I'm not losing sight of him again, not if I can help it. I'm hovering right over him, gliding with my talons actually touching the waves, keeping pace with him as he struggles to make progress through the sea with the yagi mobbing him, pulling him down.

Besides his sheer size and heaviness, I'm reluctant to try to pick him up because, as I just mentioned, dragon talons are one of the few things that can pierce dragon armor (on the underbelly only, or if we're not all the way changed over from human).

If Ed was a relatively skinny person, I could wrap my toes around him so that only the fleshy parts touched him, and the talons would link like a belt-buckle in front of him, and he'd be fine. It's a tricky move insofar as there's grave potential for stabbing, but when executed properly, it *can* work.

But I don't know anything about picking up a hydra. He's big enough around in his current form that my talons would dig right into him. I don't know if his scales can resist them, or if I'd be stabbing him through ten times over.

So while I'm coasting above him, debating what to do and generally watching him closely so I don't lose him again, he breaches a second time, this leap not quite so high, but high enough to bring him up right under my belly.

And at the same time as he's doing that, he starts to change from a hydra to a man.

His flippers turn to arms with hands, and he grabs hold of one of my legs even as he's still losing his long hydra tail.

The sudden weight tugs me instantly downward, and I strain to fly high enough to keep him out of the reach of the six-handed yagi.

I *have* to keep him out of their grasp. He's terribly vulnerable in human form.

Ed pulls himself up my leg, hand over hand, like he's climbing a rope.

I beat my wings hard just to fly a little higher, out of reach of the yagi, but not so high we could be easily seen. Not like I could fly that high, anyway. I was tired before. And now I have a heavy Scotsman clinging to my legs, dragging me down even more than he would tucked into an aerodynamically less-disruptive spot behind my neck.

Not that I'm complaining. Not at all. I'm relieved, more relieved than I can put into words.

It's just that we're in the middle of the Black Sea in the middle of the day, with nowhere to go and no strength to get there even if I had somewhere to go.

We can't go down to the water again or the yagi will swarm us. We can't fly on, continuing east along our intended route, because I will die of exhaustion long before we ever make it to shore.

The only other option is to turn sharply south toward Turkey, except that I'm a dragon in dragon form and its broad daylight. The sun is high above us. It won't be getting dark out for many hours yet. It's not safe to head toward land.

But where else can I go?

Chapter Twelve

I veer southward toward the Turkish mainland. It's not a good option, but everything else is worse. There are a few billowy clouds ahead, and I point my nose toward them as I beat my wings, struggling to keep the two of us high enough above the water that the yagi can't grab Ed away from me.

The clouds may offer me a bit of cover, but at the same time, they'll blind me to anything else around me.

I study the shore. I can see far up and down the coastline in either direction. There are piers, villages, beaches, and resorts.

But in between those, here and there, I also see miles of coastline with jagged cliffs, with thick trees above and sharp rocks below. Maybe, if I'm particularly lucky, I can find a stretch of cliffs inaccessible by road.

Making note of the most promising cliffs, I beat my wings toward the clouds and enter the thick mist. The beads of airborne water are cool on my skin, and I open my mouth wide, letting the humidity coat my tongue, the closest thing I have to a drink of water, considering that the Black Sea, besides being thick with yagi, is salty.

Then I focus all my strength on keeping us aloft, headed toward the cliffs. I am *so* exhausted. I thought I was tired the other night, but that was nothing. My muscles are sore, aching, in places screaming in pain with every flap of my wings. On top of that, I'm afraid Ed might slip out of my grasp at any moment, even though I'm not so much holding on to him as he is holding on to me.

It's all I can do to fly toward the stretch of cliffs.

Toward the stretch of cliffs.

I can't see them. I can't see anything but disorienting whiteness all around, and glimpses of the sea between wisps of white below. I fly based on my internal sense of direction and my memory of where the cliffs were before I entered the clouds.

My wings are aching. I beat them strategically, timing my wing flaps and angling my body to use the least amount of energy while coasting the greatest distance.

Not that I can coast very far with Ed clinging to my legs. But if he tried to climb up onto my back, he'd only disrupt my gliding even more, and I think he realizes that. Or else he, too, is too tired to move any more than he absolutely has to.

The clouds break apart below us and I realize we've lost altitude. We're in the open again, my feet inches above the water. I glance around for any sign we might be seen, panicked enough I'm fully awake now. To my relief, there are no boats right here, as the rocks protrude far out to sea from the coast.

The cliffs are not far in front of me—less than a mile. That is the good news.

The bad news is that they are high, so very high. I can barely keep my toes above the water. I can't imagine flying high enough to reach the tree-shaded woods atop the cliffs.

Instead, I drag myself forward, beating my aching wings, determined to keep Ed above the rocks that jut up from the sea all around us. Soon there are more rocks than sea, and I feel the release of a heavy weight, realizing full seconds later, in my stupor, that Ed has let go and landed amidst the rocky outcroppings that litter the space between the land and the sea.

It occurs to me that I have no more reason to keep flying. We're not technically to land yet but we are among the rocks, and I'm too tired to care anymore, anyway.

I land, changing into human form and slumping down on a slab of rock in a sliver of shade from a tall boulder, and letting my body sink into the grasping claws of sleep.

"Wren, open yer mouth a bit, can ye?"

Unsure if Ed's voice is real or if I'm dreaming, I open my mouth.

"Drink." Ed's got his water bottle pressed to my lips. I drink in slow sips, then slip back into the fog of sleep.

Who-knows-how-long later, when Ed's voice again rouses me, this time with the offer of fish to eat, I open one eye just far enough to look around, and see that Ed's moved me under the cliffs to a place where the beating waves have carved a shallow cavity from the cliff wall. It's not quite what I'd call a proper *cave*, but it's enough to keep us out of sight from the sides and above. Considering how far the rocks stretch out in front of us, both above and below the water, I doubt any boat will get close enough to land to see us.

We're safe, at least from humans.

I eat the fish.

Ed shares his water bottle with me.

"I'm surprised you still have water," I mumble, thinking out loud.

"We drank it all, aye," Ed explains, "but I walked the coast a bit—wanted to make sure we weren't going to be spotted. No one for miles on either side, but there was a trickle of waterfall down that way a bit, so I refilled me bottle."

"Good idea. But weren't you tired?"

"Aye. But not so tired as ye, and I thought it necessary."

Eating has lifted me from my stupor, and I adjust myself, trying to find a comfortable resting position among the rocks. I'd like to lean back against something, but everything is lumpy and jagged and set at wrong angles. My muscles were sore enough before. Now they're extra achy from the cold hard stones.

"Something troublin' ye?" Ed asks as I shift and wince.

Every position I try seems to jab at bruises and tender places I didn't know I had. "The rocks are painful."

"Here's a smooth spot." Ed sweeps one hand across the level surface beside him. "You can lean on me."

Part of me doesn't think I should get any closer to Ed than I already have, but another part of me wants to be close to him. More than either of those opinions, though, is my all-consuming need to rest, preferably in a position that's not utterly painful.

I join him on the flat slab of rock, and he wraps one arm around my shoulders as I lean back against his chest. My legs are sticking out sideways from the direction of his legs, and he's propped against a boulder which I can't imagine being any more comfortable than anything I tried to lean against, but he doesn't seem to mind and for all I know he's a different creature than I am, anyway. Maybe hydras like resting against hard rocks.

With that uncertainty swirling through my thoughts, I fall asleep.

Normally, when I'm exhausted from being a dragon, I sleep a hard, dreamless sleep. Maybe it's because I don't feel safe here, on the edge of the sea where the yagi might still attack us, or maybe my subconscious is trying to process all the questions churning in my thoughts, but my sleep isn't dreamless.

It's fitful and fearful. I'm fighting yagi. I'm in the water. They're pulling me down. I don't know who Ed is, and I can't find him, but if I can't find him I'll never know who he was. I'll never know what I missed. I'll miss out on something important. Ed is important, but the yagi are pulling him away from me, deeper and deeper into the dark water. I can't reach him. He's gone.

"Eeeed!" I'm calling out his name, trying to find him, when I awaken.

His face is close to mine. "Shh, hush now, yer fine. I'm here. Hush."

It's dark out. Night. Maybe we should take advantage of the darkness and try to travel toward Azerbaijan, but I'm too exhausted to make it far and I doubt we'd find as good a resting spot as this, not without going out of our way.

My heart is pounding from the struggle in my dreams. I breathe slowly in and out.

"Yer fine, Wren. Yer safe," Ed whispers in soothing tones.

I listen to his words, focusing on the calming rumble of his voice, both as his breath whispers past my ear and his chest echoes beneath my other ear. It's like a weird surround sound, one ear treble, the other bass. Slowly the meaning of his words sink in.

I'm safe.

"Ye 'wake now?" Ed asks.

"Was I dreaming?"

"Sounded like a nightmare to me."

Panic seeps through my muddled thoughts. Who knows what I might have said in the midst of my troubled dreams. I was so worried about Ed, about losing him—I didn't give away feelings that aren't necessarily real, did I? "Did I say anything?"

"Ye were shoutin' for me, like I was getting pulled down by those creatures yesterday. That scare ye, did it?"

"Yes. It scared me a lot." I'm wide awake now.

"Scared me, too. I understand why yer afeared of deep water, the way those devils pull ye down. But I got away. Thanks to yer help. Don't know as I'd have made it otherwise."

I bury my face closer against his shoulder. I've got one arm slung around him already, but now I hold him tight, still terrified by how close he came to getting pulled under for good.

"What were those devils?" Ed asks. "Same thing as attacked ye in the Caspian Sea?"

"Yes. The same exact thing." I suppress a shudder, and then tell him everything I know—about Eudora, the regular yagi, and my theories about these new adversaries, which I've dubbed water yagi, for clarity's sake. And while I'm on the subject of Eudora, I fill Ed in on her history, including the fact that my mother made her fully human a little over two decades ago—which is why, in addition to wanting to destroy all dragons generally, she has a particular hatred for our family.

As I might have expected, Ed takes an immediate and strong dislike to Eudora. "I canna see why she's been let live. At the very least, she ought to be imprisoned where she can wreak no harm."

101

"We've got spies watching her, but that's about the best we can do. It's too dangerous to attempt a direct attack. There aren't many dragons in the world. We can't afford to lose any."

"I'd fight her," Ed murmurs, his body tensing behind me as though he's envisioning the battle. "I'd risk my life to keep ye safe, and the waters free of these devils."

Fear for Ed's safety rushes through me. Eudora is so dangerous, and so are the yagi. I don't want anything to happen to Ed. I almost lost him out on the water.

It occurs to me that I need to know—even though I'm afraid of what I'll learn—I need to know what he is and what he capable of. Is he bullet-proof? Is he talon-proof? Not only might I rest more peacefully once I know the full truth, but we'll be able to fight more effectively. We'll make a better team.

So I take a deep breath and pose the question. "What kind of dragon are you? I mean, I know you're a hydra, but I don't know what all that means."

His chest tenses beneath me, and for a few seconds I'm afraid I've asked a question he doesn't know how to answer. He did say before that he's never met another hydra, or something like that. Is he an orphan, then? Maybe he doesn't even know what he is.

But he breathes out a slow confession. "The history of the Scottish people and the history of her dragons are intertwined more than most folks realize. Seven hundred years ago, the Scottish Highlands were thick with dragons. Every castle, every district, had a dragon king and queen and family, and they lived at peace and ruled the sky. Insofar as there was peace, it was the dragons that kept the peace. Some folks thought it shouldn't be that way—that people, not dragons, should rule."

"Are you that old?" The question escapes my mouth involuntarily.

But Ed doesn't look offended. "Nay, not quite. But me parents were. They were the dragons to who built Nattertinny castle. They ruled over the loch and the surrounding lands. So much of Scotland was built by dragons. Even the kilt was designed by us, since we kept splitting our pants when we changed into dragons. Mighty sensible in design, kilts are, for dragons. Humans took to wearing them as a status symbol since those in authority—the dragons—wore kilts."

The history of the kilt is interesting, but I'm still stuck on what he said just before. "Your parents were dragons?"

"Aye."

"You mean water dragons—hydras—right?"

"Nay. They were dragons, much like you, with wings to fly, and all. They could swim in the lake, too, but not like me. I never met a dragon who could hold their breath like me, or stay underwater like me. Perhaps, if they could, they'd still be alive."

Sorrow underscores his words, so I stay silent, even though questions are shouting in my mind. If Ed's parents are dragons, what happened to make him a hydra? Is he technically a dragon, too, or something else entirely?

Ed keeps on with his story. "Some folk—not just people, but dragons, too, though I don't understand how they could turn on their own kind—some folk decided dragons were too wild. Not civilized enough for the world as it was becoming. Too powerful for their own good, even. And they hunted down the dragons. They fought them and killed them.

"It was in one of these battles, while I was yet an egg, that Nattertinny Castle was attacked. Me parents were outnumbered and they fled. Me mother tried to carry me egg away to safety, but she had to fight off her attackers, and she did what she could. She dropped me egg into the loch.

"Me egg stayed in the water for three years—far longer than most eggs incubate. I suppose the cold waters sent me into a dormant state, or maybe it was my injuries that set me back. Whatever it was, me parents had been chased away. They took shelter first on the Shetland Islands, and when those were attacked, they fled to Faroe. But me mother feared for me safety all that time. She'd noted the spot where she'd dropped me egg, and eventually, when the violence against dragons died down, most of them bein' killed off or banished by this time, she sneaked back and pulled me egg from the loch.

"It had been damaged, either when it hit the water or the rocks below, or in the shiftin' currents over time. But our eggs are leathery, ye know, not so brittle as a chicken egg. In spite of the years that had passed, she held out hope I'd hatch, and I did. But me knees were bent and me hands," Ed holds them out. The night is dark, but he infuses his greenish glow in the malformed limbs, and now I understand. "They were never quite right."

I slip my hand over his and the glow dies down. He gives my fingers a familiar squeeze and continues his story.

"Some say, 'tis a dragon's wings that are the last thing to form in the egg, like a caterpillar turnin' into a butterfly. I dunno if it was the injury to me egg, or the long hibernation in the cold water, but I never got me wings." His voice is sad now, and mournful.

"Seeing as how I couldna fly, me parents feared for me safety more than most. Time passed, a generation of men came and went, and me parents took back their castle, but they knew another attack could come at any time. I loved to swim. Probably from me time marinatin' in the loch. Our eggs are porous, too, so the water got in and shaped who I am. I loved the water and I could swim as well as any dragon could fly, so we made our plan. If our castle was attacked, since I couldna fly to safety, I'd hide in the loch."

He falls silent.

I don't want to ask, but it seems almost cruel to leave him stuck in this spot, in the most painful place. "Is that what happened?"

"Aye. Me parents fought while I hid. When the battle was over, they'd slain their enemies, but me father was dead and me mother on her last breath. I did for her what I could to make her comfortable, and I got to say goodbye. 'Twas all."

I squeeze his hand again, this time a long squeeze almost like a hug. "I'm sorry."

He squeezes my hand in return. "So am I."

I feel pain for him, terrible pain at all he lost and the long loneliness he's endured since. But at the same time, the thing that's pounding in my chest isn't sorrow, but a question I'm almost too afraid to ask.

But I *have* to ask. I mean, I can almost guess at the answer already, even though it's not the answer I wanted it to be. So I have to know for sure, because otherwise I might assume the wrong thing, and maybe I am wrong, maybe I'm worried for nothing. So after a long silence in which I battle with myself over whether it's necessary to ask, and then make up my mind to do it, I finally put together some words.

"Ed?"

"Aye?"

"So does that mean, even though you don't look like a regular dragon, you're not something else? A hydra's not a separate thing? You're really a dragon?"

Chapter Thirteen

"I'm as much a dragon as ye are."

"We're the same kind, then?" My pulse is pounding through every vein in my body, screaming in a fit of silent terror he can probably feel clearly since I'm still leaning against him, my face pressed to that lovely dip between his shoulder and his chest.

"Aye." He tenses slightly beneath me, probably because of the anxiety pouring out of me. "Does that trouble ye?"

I've got to get to the bottom of this.

I don't *want* to ask.

I'm pretty sure I'm not going to like the answer, but I *have* to ask.

I have to know. Knowing might be terrible, but at least then I'll have the facts so I can figure out how to proceed. "Did you know my grandmother, Faye Goodwin?"

"Faye was yer grandmother? Aye, yea, I knew her well. Her parents and me parents were acquainted, and made provisions that she and I should be betrothed. But when she met me and saw I was damaged, she didna want me, not as a mate. We stayed on friends a bit. I hoped she might someday change her mind about me, but then she disappeared and I never learned what happened. I searched for her, but I never found her."

I'm breathing heavily now, battling these facts as hard as I fought the yagi.

Ed is a dragon.

He's the dragon my grandmother knew, the dragon we came to Scotland to find. I should probably fill him in on what happened with my grandmother, but I've got to know something else first. "Are the Sheehys dragons?"

"Nay. They're me people, the last of me parents' faithful tribe of old. They keep me castle for me and make their livin' lettin' out rooms to guests. It gives me cash flow to buy cattle without dippin' into my treasure hoard. They're good folks, but nay, they not be dragons. Yer mother asked me the same thing."

"Was that what the two of you talked about?"

"It was one thing."

"So she knows?"

"Aye, she knows, and she told me the reason for yer visit. I told her she didna hafta to stay out her reservation, now her hope of mates for yer sisters was gone. The castle gets a waiting list in season. We can let out yer rooms to someone else."

"You think she'll be heading home, then?"

"Sounded as though she might."

"I see." So, then, my mother knows. And my sisters probably know by now, too, or will know soon—maybe they weren't in on the purpose of our visit, but I'm sure they suspected something was up. And if my mother decided to cancel, she'd likely explain why.

She'd explain everything, since there would no longer be any point in keeping it a secret.

I don't like it. Zilpha will be disappointed when she learns the truth, since she'd put so much hope in finding a mate.

But the only available mate is Ed.

The truth hits me so hard I sit up straight and gasp.

"What is it?" Ed sounds alarmed.

"You could marry Zilpha!"

"Yer sister?" Ed asks, as though there might be some other dragon woman named Zilpha in need of a mate.

"Yes! She wants to marry. She wants a mate, a dragon. She wants to make dragon babies." I look at Ed. It's pretty dark out, the moon a pool of silver mirrored by the sea, the stars distant glimmers winking at us between wisps of cloud, so I can't see his face clearly. But what I can see does not look nearly as happy or relieved as I might expect of a man who wanted to marry years ago but was shut down and now finally has a chance.

If anything, he looks…sad?

I squeeze Ed's hand. "Don't you want to marry and make dragon babies?"

"Aye. Been wantin' that for many a century." But he still doesn't sound happy or relieved, and his eyes, which were glowing with vibrant color moments ago, fade until I can hardly see their light. He turns his face away from me. His voice has gone cold and distant, like the depths of Loch Ness.

I'm not sure why he sounds that way. What could possibly make him anything but thrilled at this moment, when the thing he's been wanting for so long is now within his grasp? I grapple to find a reason. "Biologically speaking, that's something you can do, right?"

"Aye. All I lack is a willing mate."

"Zilpha is a willing mate. An *eager* and willing mate."

"I dunno that she seemed keen on me."

"That's only because she didn't know there was a mate available, or if she had figured it out, she thought the Sheehy brothers were dragons. Once she finds out *you're* the dragon, she'll be keen on you." I squeeze his hand again and try to stop my nervous babbling. "Come on, then. It's a great idea, right?"

"Nay. I appreciate your concern, but I do not want to marry yer sister." Ed's voice is still cold, edged with pain.

I don't understand. "Why not?"

"Because." He turns to face me and looks into my eyes. His are green and lovely and lit like gemstones with a fire from within, glowing much brighter now, so that I can see his face, or as much of it as isn't covered by beard. "Wren? I love ye."

I drop Ed's hand as if I've been stung. I may have even given a little yelp.

Maybe more of a scream.

Judging my Ed's expression, it was a scream.

Hopefully I didn't sound too terrified. I don't want to hurt his feelings.

Too late. The glow leaves his eyes and he turns his head away.

I don't know what to say to him. What can I say? *Don't take it personally? It's not you, it's me?* Considering how long Ed's been around, he's probably heard those lines before. I can't do that to him.

But what can I say?

"I'm sorry," I tell him.

"Nay," he doesn't look at me. "I'm sorry. I should not have said anythin'. We were gettin' along fine and now..."

"No, it's my fault. I pushed you to say it. I should have kept my mouth shut. I just didn't think you were going to say *that*."

He looks back at me, but the darkness hides his expression. "I thought I'd communicated as much these last few days, takin' care of ye, and all. I guess I dunno how that works."

I stare at him a long time as the truth soaks in. Yes, of course Ed loves me. How could I not see that? He's been attentive to my every need, he's been gentle and sweet and considerate. Maybe he hasn't done the typical love things like bringing me flowers or chocolate, but he's given me raw fish and headless cattle. For dragons, that's much the same thing.

He's told me he loved me in every way but with words.

And maybe, I realize with regret, thinking back to the many times I've held his hands and leaned on the comforting strength of his shoulder, maybe I've been telling him, in every way but with words, that I feel the same way.

Even though I don't.

I can't. I mean, I. Just. Can't.

Something wrenches inside me, more painful than tired muscles or a rock-sore seat. I can't love Ed. He wants to marry and I don't want to marry. He wants dragon babies and I don't even want to think about wanting dragon babies. I've been taking advantage of his kindness, letting him fight my enemies for me, letting the yagi drag him down into the sea in my place, but I can't love him.

But before I can attempt to explain any of this to Ed, he stands.

I haul myself to my feet beside him. "Where are you going?"

"Shh. I thought I heard somethin'." He's looking out to sea, past the rocks, into the vast blackness, dark waves tipped with silvery moonlight.

I see nothing but endless ripples and waves.

"Get the knives out the backpack," Ed whispers softly as he draws the broadsword from its scabbard.

I need to talk to him, to explain where I'm coming from and assure him my feelings aren't anything personal, to fill him in on my grandmother's choice, as well, which I understood to be about her own position, not wanting to be a dragon at all anymore, rather than a response to his deformity.

But before I can say anything, the sea breeze carries a hint of an odor that's different from the brine of the sea.

Sea yagi.

Their stench is a little like the regular yagi and a little like the worst low tide odor ever. I'm far, far more familiar with it by now than I ever wanted to be.

I step back toward our bags and pull out the weapons we brought, which seem so feeble compared to real swords. But they'll have to be enough.

It's all we have.

I put the knives—long, dagger-like knives with blades nearly a foot long—on a rock, then slip the backpacks on over my shoulders, glancing about to make sure we haven't left anything behind. Ed's got the water bottle clipped to a loop on his kilt. We've got everything we brought, if we need to make a quick exit.

Gripping the knives, one in each hand, I walk back and stand beside Ed, facing the lake, staring out at sea, studying each glimmer to determine whether it's water or yagi.

The first one leaps from behind a boulder. It's closer to me, but Ed steps toward it and severs its head in a single slash.

I'm impressed. The seam between the head and body of the yagi is a narrow gap hardly big enough for a sword. You have to hit it at just the right angle. It took me years of practice to learn to execute regular yagi properly, and a bit of adjustment to adapt the move to sea yagi.

Ed got it right on his first try. But then, I figure he's probably had decades, even centuries of practice with that sword, even if he wasn't using it to fight yagi.

The next creature bounds through the darkness from Ed's other side. With only one sword, he has to swing it across his body. The blade glances off the yagi armor once, twice, before severing the head.

By now I can hear them coming, even if I can't see them in the darkness. I hear the clatter of their exoskeletons and smell their stench.

And then they swarm, pouring over the rocks in streams, balancing on their two feet, clambering with their extra sets of hands, grasping, grasping, too many hands. I'm slashing, trying to aim, lunging to reach them since the knives are shorter than the swords I'm used to.

With two knives, I adapt my swing. Instead of beheading two at a time, I lunge right, then left, then right again, whipping my blades and ducking back to behead another. It's an effective maneuver, though I wince each time at how close I have to be before I can use the short blades, and the water yagi are crawling up from the sea in ever-larger numbers.

I miss my swords.

Ed moves further away from me as he swings his mighty broadsword. I understand that he doesn't want me too close to the powerful blade in action, but I still feel exposed without him at my back.

When steaming yagi heads are as numerous as the stones as our feet, as the yagi pour forth faster, I leap atop a tall rock and scream to Ed. "We've got to get out of here!"

"How?"

I look out to sea. The water is vast, immense, filled with many yagi. I decapitate two more as I make my decision.

I'm not going out there.

"Ride on my back!"

"Yer too tired."

The yagi are swarming thick around me. "Just get over here!" I shriek. I can't argue any longer, but swell and change, growing into a dragon.

Ed bounds across the rocks and leaps onto my back.

He is so heavy.

I strain upward. Taking off from low ground with no wind is always hardest, besides which these are water yagi we're fighting. They grab my talons and cling to me and try to pull me down. I kick my legs and fling them away, lifting off, circling wide over the rocky shore, catching what little sea breeze I can find, fighting gravity and exhaustion as I circle back again, three times around in circles as I slowly glide and climb, each inch higher a strain on my sinews, until I'm high enough to top the sheer cliff.

We land among the trees. I can go no farther, but change back into my human self.

Ed props me up and I cling to him, never mind that less than an hour ago he told me he loves me and I told him I don't love him back, and clinging to his shirtless chest is probably not the best way to reinforce my detachment. I simply cannot hold myself up without him. I need his strength.

"Think we'll be safe up here?" I ask, panting.

"That's a steep cliff, close to a hundred feet high, with nothing to hold on to climbing up," Ed assures me, and I recall that he explored the area before it grew dark. "There's no way up that I could see. We're safe from them, but I don't know what else might be up here."

I nod, but on the inside I'm not so sure. If the yagi are part octopus or squid, who's to say they can't climb up the cliff like a spider? I don't think they have suction cups on their hands, but neither can I rule it out.

I'm struggling to catch my breath, and maybe some of the raggedness of my breathing is due to my shaky emotional state. Ed is way nicer to me than he needs to be. If you've been keeping track, he declared his love for me, and I rebuffed him, and then he fought yagi to keep me safe and he worried that I would be too tired to escape (which I essentially was, so you can't fault his assessment), and now he's holding me close when he could be pushing me away and pouting.

Ed is not a pouter. I appreciate that about him.

I also feel guilty.

"Thank you," I whisper, holding him tight as I prop myself against him.

"For what?"

"For letting me lean on you," I'm panting, trying to find words and catch my breath at the same time, "even though I don't love you back."

"I didna ask ye to love me back. Nor do I expect it." He adjusts his arms around me so I can stand a little taller with my weight still slumped against him.

His words are confusing.

"What do you mean?" I ask.

"I'm damaged. Faye didna want me. I didna expect as anyone would."

"It's not that! I like your hands the way they are. And while, yes, maybe it would be helpful if you had wings to fly, still, you can swim like nobody else, and that's just as good in its own way. You're not *damaged*. You're just different. Besides that, I don't know what my grandmother told you, but she had issues of her own. She didn't even want to be a dragon at all, so the last thing she wanted was to bring more dragons into the world."

"I know she didna want to be a dragon," Ed acknowledges. "It was the being hunted that she couldna stand. She was a social butterfly, as ye might say. She wanted people to like her. Being a dragon got in the way of that. I'm no butterfly. We were two different people. Best we didna try to marry, I suppose.

"All that aside," he continues, "I didna mean to raise the subject of marriage. I gave up that hope long ago. 'Tis a gift to know another dragon at all. I'm honored to be yer friend. Don't let the depth of my feelin's get in the way of that. Please."

His words stir something inside of me. My mom and my sisters have been so focused on their plans to find a mate, it didn't occur to me that Ed might not have the same goal. "Can we still be friends, then?"

Chapter Fourteen

Ed smiles so broadly, I can see it in spite of the near-darkness of the pre-morning hour. "Aye. I want nothin' more."

I hug him, then. Technically we were probably mostly hugging already, but I tighten my grip around him as waves of gratitude radiate from me. Ed is way, way too good to me. Aside from my sisters, he's probably the best friend I've ever had, even if I've only known him a few days. Sure, I've had friends—both those in the Azeri village who knew I was a dragon, and those in the states who didn't. But none of them understood me the way Ed understands me.

"Want me to hunt up something to eat?" Ed asks after a few minutes.

See, I told you he understands me.

"I'm wary about venturing too far."

"It's coming on morning here. The animals will stir in the cool of the day. If I'm to hunt us anythin' to eat, now's the time. I won't go far, but ye need yer strength. Besides of which, I should have a look around to see if there be anyone about. Best to do that before full light."

"Wait. I have an idea." I dig around in my backpack and am relieved to discover that in spite of all it's been through, my tablet is still safe and dry inside its sturdy waterproof case. "I haven't needed to use this because I've known where we were up until now. But I don't know if I have maps loaded for this area. We're further south than I thought we'd be, and I'm pretty sure there's no Wi-Fi out here."

Ed watches the screen from behind my shoulder as the images load.

"Here we are. Blue triangle." There's not much detail in this area, but the towns and roads are noted. We're roughly halfway across the Black Sea, where the southern coast bulges northward. While there's a road that follows the coast in many places, it veers inland in the area where we are—probably because of the dangerous cliffs. "I can't tell what you might find for houses and people around, but there aren't any towns or roads."

"That's useful knowledge. I'll be careful. Ye need yer rest." Ed helps me find a decent spot to lie down, out of sight behind some rocks and bushes. It's not the most comfortable bed, but it's better than the hard rocks below, and I'm so tired it doesn't much matter as long as I can close my eyes.

The sky is getting lighter by the minute. While I stretch out with my head on one backpack and a knife close at hand beside me (we may be a hundred feet above the yagi, but I don't trust them to stay away), Ed slips away through the trees to find us something to eat.

How long I sleep, I'm not sure, but the full light of morning has dawned when Ed awakens me to a meal of roasted venison.

"We'll have to lay low here for the day," he informs me solemnly as he shares the meat. "This area is not so sparsely populated as what we're used to. Best we not venture from this spot. We can sleep through the heat of the day. Will ye be able to fly tonight?"

"I don't have much choice," I acknowledge between bites. "We can stay close to the coast, but we've got to keep going. Even if we only make it part way, we'll stay ahead of the yagi, at least."

We finish the meal in silence. I'm too tired to talk. When I'm done eating, I brush my teeth with a bit of water from Ed's water bottle, and then stretch out on the ground again.

Ed disposes of the bones from our meal. Then he settles in to sleep several feet away from me.

I'm not quite asleep yet. Part of me has stayed awake, alert to his movements, waiting for him to stretch out near me. When I watch him lie down far beyond the reach of my arms, I feel a burst of disappointment so strong it startles me.

Why do I feel so disappointed?

It's not as though I'd be that much safer with Ed a few feet closer to me. Technically I'm probably safer with him nearer the cliffs, where the yagi would encounter him first if they figured out how to climb up to us.

And what do I expect from Ed, really?

He told me he loves me. I denied loving him. I essentially told him to back off.

He's only doing what I told him to do.

So why do I feel so disappointed?

*

We awake at sundown and walk to the edge of the cliff, where I stretch my aching wings and swell into a form it exhausts me to inhabit. Ed climbs onto my back and I hop from the cliff, expecting to drop like a rock from the weight I'm carrying, but a steady updraft lifts me.

Once I'm free of the cliffs and the trees, I can feel the breeze, a constant breeze that grows stronger the higher I fly. And it's blowing in the direction of home.

I could weep with gratitude.

Instead, I set my course due east, toward the northern mountains of Azerbaijan, and fly as fast as my wings will let me. True, it's tiring to fly fast rather than simply glide, but I don't know how long this gift of a tailwind will last. I'm going to take it as far and as fast as it will allow me. Once it's gone, I'll have to work far harder just to make a fraction as much progress.

Soaring at such a speed, within a couple of hours I can see the twinkling lights of the resorts and towns on the eastern shore of the Black Sea. I hadn't expected to make it this far before morning, and had fully anticipated being too weak to continue flying by the time I reached the mountains beyond the towns.

But now, as I approach the coast, the wind still strong at my back, pushing me toward home, I see no reason not to go on. I need to talk to my dad, to find out what he knows about the water yagi, and to share what Ed and I have learned about them. And it would be nice to sleep in my own bed instead of on the hard ground.

So I keep flying, past the coast, over the first ridge of mountains, toward home.

The nearer I get, the more I start to formulate a plan for my arrival.

My village and the home I was raised in, are further east than my grandfather's village where my mother grew up. My father and grandfather are dragon kings of neighboring kingdoms—not that these kingdoms are politically recognized in any formal sort of way today. Their kingdoms are more like what modern folks might think of as a tribe or region. But those tribes date back thousands of years, beyond human memory and even dragon memory.

I'm going to have to fly over my grandfather's village to get home. It's really no big deal, there's no danger, or anything. I mean, I can't wait to get home, and all that. It's just that someone's bound to see me and call over to my hometown to let them know I'm on my way.

Not that I really expected to sneak in unnoticed. But they'll probably line the streets to welcome me home, and there's going to be a big deal, all of which embarrasses me on a good day. But even that's not so bad compared to seeing my sisters.

Because if Ed's guess is right and my mom and sisters head home, they'll be arriving soon, if they're not already be there (they haven't had to carry a heavy hydra, which means they could fly much further and faster, and that's not even factoring in the time they'll save not having to fight water yagi). Don't get me wrong—I love my mother and sisters.

I'm just not sure if I'm ready to see them yet. Especially because my sisters are going to be pretty bummed that things didn't work out with the Sheehy brothers. And I feel guilty about flying off with the real dragon before either of them got a chance to know him, even if none of us knew what I was doing at the time.

But I need to make things right. Zilpha wants so much to marry. I know Ed said he didn't think she was that keen on him, but he has no idea how important marriage is to her. Once she realizes Ed's the real dragon, not Angus or Magnus, I know she'll be keen on Ed right quick.

So I've got to give the two of them the opportunity to get to know each other and fall in love and all that. If you think about it, the only real reason Ed likes me is because I'm a dragon. And Zilpha is also a dragon. So they should have no problem falling in love.

This is what I want. I want Ed to be happy. Zilpha wants to marry. Ed does, too. They can make each other happy. And I will be happy just knowing they're happy. I'm sure of it.

I'm just not looking forward to starting that process.

Not quite yet.

The mountains are dark and thick, and even the villages nestled in the valleys are mostly dark at this hour. But this is my homeland and I could find my way through these rugged peaks in pitch blackness, if I had to. I sweep over the last major valley. I'm starting to feel my exhaustion in every muscle again, but I'm so close to home after such a long journey, I ignore the pain and press on.

The mountains are dark shadows with the pale pre-light of dawn backlighting their shapes in the sky. I fly faster, like a sprint to the finish. I recognize the peaks, the cliff sides, the mountain streams, the final wall of stone that makes my grandfather's village so nearly inaccessible from outside, and then I'm over the last mountain.

And there it is, my grandfather's village. I swoop wide, past the town just awakening to the light of dawn. Maybe, if I'm quick, people won't see me, or won't get the news forwarded to my village in time to assemble a welcoming party.

I speed toward my home village, pull up and land on the King's Tower, the ancient entrance to the town, with its wide parapets built expressly for landing dragons (my grandfather's village has one of these, too. Long ago they were as common as dragons). I land on the stones and shrink back into human form.

Ed's feet touch the stone floor as I shrink, and he spins, his arms still around me. He switches seamlessly from holding onto me, to holding me up.

I lean against his shoulder. As always, I'm exhausted and grateful for his support. But I cling to him for another reason, too.

This is the end of our journey. Not the end of our mission, of course—we've still got to figure out where the yagi are coming from and how to make them go away for good. I don't even want to think about the yagi right now, because they first showed up in the Caspian Sea, and now we've encountered them in large numbers in the Black Sea as well.

How long before they're everywhere, before no water is safe from them?

How long will it be before even Loch Ness is too dangerous for Ed or any dragon to swim there?

No, I don't want to think about that, and my heart is full, anyway, with the realization that this time I've spent together with Ed, just the two of us, is over. I'm going to go on with my life and he's going to go on with his, hopefully with Zilpha at his side.

Happily ever after, just the way she's always wanted it.

"Ye all right?" Ed asks.

"Fine." I inform him, sniffing back—what the! Are those? No, they can't be. I'm not crying. I do not cry. Especially not over something mushy like coming home after a long journey or leaving a guy who has only ever been just a friend.

120

Ed runs his rough fingers across my cheek, brushing away moisture. "'Twas a long flight. Ye did mighty well. I didna expect ye to make it all the way here in one night."

"It was exhausting," I admit, ready to claim his interpretation, even if it's not exactly true. I don't cry from exhaustion. But if it's true I'm crying (Ed wipes more tears from my other cheek. It's true.), I'd rather he think it's from exhaustion, and not anything…personal.

"Now what do we do?" Ed asks.

"There are doors on either side of the tower with changing rooms below. Men's" I point past him, "and women's," I gesture behind me. "There are robes in there. Pick one. We also had bathrooms put in a few years ago. I'm going to brush my teeth. And my hair." I reach up toward my dark locks. They're not exactly wind-whipped, since I had scales instead of hair as I flew, but they're not exactly smooth, either. "Then you go down the stairs and out the front door."

"Ah. I see." Ed answers politely, though the look in his eyes says his question wasn't so much about the next practical steps for entering the city, but has something more to do about us.

Now what do we do?

I understand the question, but I don't have an answer for it.

"Wren?" Ed smooths his hand along my cheek again. I'm pretty sure I got the tears under control. He's not wiping anything away. His emerald eyes are studying my face with a kind of concern and attention that makes me want to tear up again. And what is it about his hands? They look so rough, but they feel so gentle against my skin.

"What?" I don't have the vocal strength to actually speak the word. It's just a whisper.

"Thank ye for all ye've done. 'Twas a gift to spend these days with ye. A precious gift."

I have to go now. I was going to stand here leaning silently on Ed's shoulder for a while longer, but not if he's going to get all sappy on me.

121

My feet are unsteady as I step away from him. "I'll meet you at the bottom of the stairs."

I don't look at him again—I can't. Instead I turn and stumble into my changing room, where I splash cold water on my face several times over, not that it really helps. And then I find a stiff canvas robe (don't we have any burlap?) and make my way down the stairs, gripping the handrail as I spiral around the tower, until I reach the bottom.

Chapter Fifteen

Ed is standing in front of the door looking out the peephole window.

"Ready?" I ask.

He turns to face me, his eyes slightly rounder than usual. "There be people out there."

"Yes. They turn out to welcome us home. It's a tradition." I cross the small room and peer out the peephole.

Immediately I understand Ed's concern. We didn't even come close to sneaking in unnoticed. There are people—a lot of people—more than usual, even—lining the sides of the street that runs through the center of the village to my childhood home at the opposite end. There are probably more people than Ed has seen in one place…ever? I don't know.

I slip my hand into his. "You can do this."

He stares at the door, and I can see the battle he's waging inside. He is a big tough guy. Wise and capable and strong. He's overcome many trials and lasted far longer than nearly all the other dragons in the world.

And right now, he'd much rather be hiding at the bottom of Loch Ness, than walking down this street filled with people happy to see him.

"Come on. I don't want them to worry."

Ed winces.

"I'll keep hold of your hand."

"Ye'll hold me hand?" His pale face regains a measure of its color.

I can't help smiling at the note in his voice, part eagerness, part relief.

"Ye won't let go?"

"Not until we're inside my house." I'm not sure why there are so many people lining the street to welcome us home. Granted, I haven't been home from school yet for summer break, so it's been months since anyone's seen me. But there really is a crowd out there, growing bigger even as we stall. They're not here to see Ed, are they? They wouldn't know about him unless my mom and sisters came home and told them. News travels quickly in our intimate village, but it has to start somewhere.

Which means they probably beat us home.

"Ready?"

"What am I supposed to do?"

"Just walk with me. Smile and wave, if you can. It'll be fun."

Ed looks unconvinced. "Not my kind of fun." But he takes a deep breath and opens the door.

The crowd raises a cheer as we step out together, my coarse-woven geometrically-patterned robe a splash of color, lime-green and brown and teal, next to the simple but soft navy blue terrycloth robe Ed chose for himself.

I wave at the people with my one free hand, and children squeal with delight and people shout words of welcome. I recognize the faces of many friends, and might have stopped to hug them or even chat, except that Ed is grapping my hand with a pressure that communicates urgency.

I glance up at his face. His expression is solemn. He nods greetings, acknowledging those who shout their welcome, but he's got his free hand tucked up into his sleeve, and when he tries to smile, his face looks pained.

I give his hand what I hope is a reassuring squeeze, and he looks down at me.

I'm still smiling, probably beaming, because in spite of my general embarrassment, in many ways I do love coming home and being greeted like this, and seeing my friends and so many familiar faces.

Ed looks at me for one long second, and then he smiles, too. A genuine, if self-conscious smile.

124

The people cheer louder.

I squeeze his hand again, and we walk briskly toward the house where I was raised, a granite fortress tucked securely against the side of a mountain—carved into the hill itself, in places.

My family is waiting there on the steps—my father, Ram, and my brothers, Ram and Felix. My mom and my sisters are there, too. Mom is the first one to break away and scoop me into a hug.

"We were worried about you. Why didn't you call?"

"Cell phone reception sucks in the Black Sea." I shrug. "I didn't think you'd be worried." I don't tell her that we were too busy fighting yagi and trying to sleep off overwhelming exhaustion to even think about what day it was, let alone whether too many days had passed, and if my folks might be worried. "Besides, phone calls aren't secure."

"You could have at least texted to let us know you're alive."

"I'm alive." I waver unsteadily and yawn. The excitement of the welcome-home parade is wearing off quickly, leaving only fatigue. "I need a nap. Food."

"Come inside." Mom leads me and Ed in through the wide doorway, and my siblings hug me and ask questions about where I've been.

Thankfully, Ed is willing to answer, in spite of the fact that the seven members of my family constitute a fairly large crowd, in Ed terms. But maybe, having just passed through the throngs that lined the main street of our village, seven doesn't seem like so many.

My mother has already told my family members who Ed is, and they listen to him with a level of respect usually reserved for my father or grandfather.

I lean against Ed's arm, not just holding his hand but propping myself against him. He's got his free hand around my waist, keeping me from sagging into a snoring puddle on the floor.

Ed's explaining to them about the water yagi, about how they attacked us in the Black Sea. That they weren't just a figment of my imagination. They're real.

Through my mostly-closed eyes I catch a glimpse of my dad's face. He looks sincerely concerned, like maybe the worst of his fears have been realized.

Then my mom returns with roast pork (she must have stepped away—I was too tired to notice) and she leads us to the dining room, where I wash down a heaping serving of meat with iced tea before I nearly choke on my drink. Even my throat is too tired to constrict in even rhythm.

"Sorry," I apologize as my sisters hand over their napkins, and I mop at the front of my robe. "I'm too tired to eat."

"I'll help you to bed," my mom offers. She supports my arm (I'm so tired I don't even know if I could make it to my room without her help) and I give Ed one last look before I retreat.

He's watching me go, his green jeweled eyes brimming with something like concern and affection, I'm not sure. I'm too sleepy to sort it out right now.

*

Next thing I know my sisters are in my room hauling me out of bed and pulling dresses from my closet and chattering all crazy excited. A glance at the clock tells me I slept away most of the day.

Rilla holds up a fluttery hunter green chiffon dress I've never worn on account of it's not remotely practical, what with its low draped back and teensy spaghetti straps. There's no way to wear a bra with it.

"This one! Perfect!" Rilla holds it up to me as Zilpha props me upright next to the bed.

I'm shaking my head, but Zilpha's squealing and even starts clapping, which leaves me unsupported.

I make a move for the bed. If I can just get under the covers without them noticing, maybe they'll forget about me and I can go back to sleep.

But Zilpha grabs my shoulder. "Come on, Wren. You've got to shower and get ready for dinner."

"Too tired. I'll eat leftovers later."

Rilla waves the dress at me, urging me toward the bathroom. "You have to come to dinner. We're all going to be there. We're going to talk about the water yagi and what to do about them. Ed's going to be there."

Ed's going to be at dinner? This only makes sense now that I think about it. Ed will be there…as will both of my sisters. This is my chance to help Ed fall in love with one of them instead of me. I have a job to do. Someone's got to play matchmaker.

"Fine." I drag myself to the bathroom. I can do this.

For my sisters.

For Ed.

*

Less than an hour later I'm sitting at the dinner table waiting for everyone else to join us for the meal. I'm wearing the hunter green dress, but only because my sisters are both wearing fancy dresses, and I don't want them to look out of place.

We don't usually dress up for supper. While we're technically princesses and my dad is the dragon king, and all that, we're normally not that weird. It's just that sometimes my mom gets it into her head that it's a special occasion, like for holidays and birthdays and when we're all home together after my sisters and I have been away at school.

And since Ed is dining with us—our first dragon guest ever besides my grandfather, who's also joining us—that makes it a very special occasion, indeed. So special my sisters curled their hair and threatened to curl mine, too, but fortunately by then we were running out of time, and I told them they had to pick between hair and makeup, so of course they went with makeup, because with our Azeri eyelashes we can do amazing things with mascara.

So I'm sitting here looking at my plate and wondering if it would be dreadfully uncomfortable to use it as a pillow, since I'm still tired and we've been waiting for at least three minutes now, when I hear the distant echo of voices reverberating through the stone halls.

Finally, the rest of my family is on their way.

I can hear my grandfather's voice, snappy and young-sounding even though he's well over two hundred years old. Although actually, if you think about it, two hundred isn't even that old compared to however old Ed is, something like six hundred, maybe? I never did get a clear answer on that.

Not that age matters at all for dragons. We grow at a rate similar to our human counterparts, reaching full physical maturity in our mid-to-late teens. From that point on, we don't age at all. We're immortal (not invincible though, that's something else entirely). We *can* be killed, we just don't age.

While I'm thinking these things the voices draw nearer until my father and grandfather enter the room. They're wearing dinner tuxedoes and their faces are freshly-shaved. My grandfather's long dark hair is pulled back in a single braid, and my dad's shoulder-length black locks are combed back, away from his face.

My brothers enter behind them—Ram, the eldest, in a suit just like my dad's, with his hair just like my dad's. He takes his role as heir to the kingdom very seriously. In fact, about the only difference between Ram and my dad is that my brother is even more serious and even, in some ways, more mature than my dad. Not to imply that my dad isn't mature. He's extremely responsible and dependable. He's king.

It's just that my brother is even more somber and formal and straight-laced.

And then Felix, the youngest, the only one who inherited any of the Scottish coloring from my grandmother, which hit him in the form of dark auburn hair (which he keeps cut short), deep blue eyes, and a smattering of freckles across his burnished cheeks. He's got on gray slacks, a navy jacket, and a pale blue shirt with a red bow tie. It's not quite dinner apparel, but compared to some of the things he's worn to the table, it's a huge improvement over what it could be.

Felix can be a goofball. Sometimes I think he's trying to get Ram to loosen up. Or maybe he just seems comical to the rest of us because we're so used to Ram.

Behind Felix, apprehension dogging his steps, enters Ed. He's in a plaid kilt with a cropped jacket, white shirt, and bow tie. At first I'm afraid they've cut his hair, but then I realize his long red locks are only pulled back into a ponytail that makes him look like an ancient warrior. Most startling of all, his beard has been reduced to a crisp goatee that accents the angle of his jaw.

And what an angle it is.

He looks gorgeous.

And also terrified.

I rise to my feet to welcome him before he can think better of this dinner gathering and flee. In five steps I've rounded the table and linked my arm through his.

"Don't run away." I whisper. "There's going to be food."

A grin spreads across his face as he looks down at me. I'd thought, when I first saw the trimmed beard, that he looked fantastic.

He looks even better when he smiles.

For a little while, I'm not sure how long, we're just standing there looking at each other. I'm adjusting to his new look, trying to acclimate to it so that my insides will stop doing fluttery flips in his presence. And then my mom comes in and announces the meal is ready, and we should bring our plates through the kitchen, buffet-style.

I admit, this isn't a traditional Azeri meal, but that's because my mom spent most of her formative years in England. We fill our plates with different kinds of meat and a few roasted vegetables, mostly for variety and fiber and to appease my mother's guilty feelings about eating so high up the food chain.

We head back to the dining room, where my father and grandfather are already trying to sort out the business with the water yagi, which apparently Ed continued to explain to them after I went off to bed.

There's a bit of jostling for places as we take our seats. I'm trying to maneuver Ed to sit by my sisters, but Ed seems more inclined to sit by me or my brothers. I end up compromising by taking the seat next to him across the table from my sisters. At least there they can admire how handsome he is.

I'll spare you the details of the conversation that followed, because there was a lot of interrupting and talking over one another, and repeating things because of the talking over one another, but the basics are thus:

My dad's spies have seen Eudora working on something at a lake near her castle in Siberia. They weren't sure what it was. Her activity there was confusing to the spies because as far as we know, yagi are bred in a lab. But on closer inspection, they've discovered the presence of something unnatural in the lake—and it sounds like the water yagi Ed and I encountered.

We've concluded, based on that information and what Ed and I observed while fighting and fleeing from the yagi, that Eudora's created a new kind of enemy to fight us, and is breeding them or growing them or whatever, in that lake. And since we've encountered them now in the Black Sea *and* the Caspian Sea, she must be making lots of them and filling all the lakes where she thinks dragons might want to float.

But that's the end of our conclusion. Beyond that are only theories and plans and wishful thinking. We don't like the water yagi. They're crazy dangerous, bred to kill us, likely more dangerous than the original yagi. We want them gone.

130

Ed's been mostly silent through the conversation, except for when he's been directly asked a question. But now, with the basic facts established, he clears his throat. Perhaps it's because he's our honored guest, or maybe it's because he hasn't spoken much, so everyone knows he wouldn't try to say anything unless it was important, but my family actually quiets down and looks at him instead of talking over him like they talk over one another.

"If I understand correctly," Ed begins, "these yagi are bred with science and dark magic. They don't breed themselves. Eudora's got some kind of water yagi factory set up at that lake. That's where all these devils are coming from."

My family members nod, but remarkably, remain silent as Ed continues.

"I can only see one solution." Here he pauses and looks around at all of us, maybe sizing us up to gauge whether we're ready to hear his plan. We must not have looked quite ready yet, because he prefaces his words. "If we let her go on churnin' out these assassins, they'll overrun the waters and nowhere will be safe. We've got to put a stop to her so she canna make any more. I say we fly up there and destroy the operation."

Chapter Sixteen

There's silence for maybe ten full seconds after Ed finishes his speech. Everyone's either digesting his words or waiting for him to say more. But he doesn't say more.

Finally, my mom says the one thing I've been thinking, which I'm pretty sure has filled everyone else's thoughts, as well. "That would be suicide."

Ed tips his head as if to admit she may be right. "The sooner we act, the fewer water yagi in the world. If we wait for them to fill the earth, nowhere will be safe. I can use me cameras to observe them. We can learn a great deal about them before we fight them. But we've got to do somethin'."

Everybody falls silent again. If their thoughts are anything like mine, they're trying desperately to find an alternative, a way out that wouldn't require an enormous risk of dragon life. And if they're like me, they can't think of anything.

"If we're going to even consider attempting this," my brother Ram presents his thoughts with measured caution, his voice extra deep, much like my dad's. "We need to know what these creatures are capable of. We don't want to get up there, practically in Eudora's clutches, and realize we've gotten in over our heads. We need to come prepared."

Felix, ever impatient, jumps on the tails of his brother's words. "How are water yagi different from regular yagi, besides living in the sea?"

Everyone looks at me and Ed. Technically, I've rarely fought regular, land-dwelling yagi, and then mostly in the dark of night. But I *have* been told about them my whole life, and trained to defend myself against their various defenses. Which means I know a far sight more about them than Ed does, considering he didn't even know such an enemy existed until I told him about them.

132

So I prop up a couple of bread rolls. (I don't know why my mom makes them, other than old English tradition—I mean, we mostly just eat meat and the odd token veggie. Occasionally we'll stuff meat into the rolls like a sandwich, but only for variety's sake. Mostly they just sit there in baskets on the table, waiting to be used as stand-ins for yagi as the need arises.) I wiggle one roll like a hand puppet as I explain, "Water yagi have hands—six sets of hands. They're part octopus, or squid, or something. They can grab you and pull you down underwater."

My mother, who's sitting on my other side, the side closest to the bread roll representing the land yagi, taps the roll and offers, "Land yagi have insectoid claws, with talons that slice and tear flesh. They're not made to grip. Further up their arms and legs, they have spines like a cockroach. But unlike a cockroach's spines, which are just there to make them look scary, these spines contain a poisonous venom that kills slowly over the course of several days. That's how we lost our first Azi."

For a few seconds, everyone at the table observes a moment of silence for the fallen dog, who saved my mother many times over. We still have Azi's great-grand pups, including a couple of dogs currently lounging by the fireplace that spans one full wall of the dining room. One of the dogs lifts his head and gives a mournful howl, as if he understands.

The howl seems to jog my mother's memory. "Land yagi also emit a wailing sound that can have a paralyzing effect on anyone who hears it. Do the water yagi have that?"

"I can't say as I heard as much underwater." Ed makes a face that says he's trying to remember. "Sound doesna travel underwater the same way as through the air. But they might have that skill, and I just havena been in a position to hear it."

Rilla asks. "Do water yagi have venom?"

I exchange looks with Ed. "Not that I know of," I admit cautiously, "but we mostly fought them in dragon form, with armored scales, so they couldn't have hurt us even if they did."

"They're armored, too?" My father clarifies.

I nod. "The water yagi armor deflected Ed's broadsword. I can't say for sure it's bullet-proof like land yagi, but I would guess so."

Ed picks up the water yagi roll. "They can swim near-on as fast as I can. Their arms are like fins or paddles. Might have a bit of a barb on the underside, now's I think on it. And they've got teeth—rows and rows of sharp teeth, like a shark."

"Maybe that's another species they're bred from," my grandfather suggests.

"Maybe." Ed agrees. "Whatever it is, it didna pierce me scales, but if ye met up with one while ye were swimmin' in human form, that would be a far different story."

"But they don't attack normal humans, right? Just dragons, in dragon or human form?" Zilpha clarifies. "Land yagi can smell if a person's a dragon. They don't bother normal people. In fact, they hide from them."

"The same must be true of water yagi," I agree. "Considering how many there were in the Black Sea, if they attacked people instead of hiding from them, we'd have heard news reports about them by now."

"Do they have antennae horns like land yagi?" my mother asks.

"Not that I've seen," Ed answers.

"How often do they come up for air?" my brother Ram asks.

Ed looks at him, a long silent look that makes my hair prickle. I know the water yagi can stay underwater far longer than I can, but surely they have to breathe at some point.

Don't they?

"I canna say as they ever seemed to need air," Ed recalls. "But I was too busy fightin' them off to think on their habits overmuch." He turns to me. "Did ye ever see them come up for air?"

I close my eyes, picturing the roiling water and especially the long stretch when Ed and even the yagi disappeared from my sight. "Never. It's almost as though they have gills."

134

Rilla gestures despairingly, her hands in the air. "Eudora's done it this time, hasn't she? Her yagi weren't good enough because we could smell them coming. With our swords, we can decapitate them before they get close enough to inflict us with their venom or stab us through with their horns. And when we're dragons, they can't touch us at all—we're armored and we can fly. They may be able to hunt us down, but they're not likely to defeat us. But *these* creatures," she laughs helplessly and shakes her head.

Zilpha picks up Rilla's speech. "The water yagi can sneak up on us when we least expect it. They can pull us underwater and hold us down until we drown. Our fire's no good under water, and our swords are difficult to use in the water. And who knows if they have venom?"

"We'll study them with the cameras first," I remind her.

"And then what?" She asks. "At some point, if we're going to disable the operation, someone's going to have to get past them, right? They're being made in a lake, right? Somebody's going to have to swim through their water."

I shudder at the thought. Fighting the water yagi hasn't helped my fears.

Ed holds out the bread roll and tears it in half. "I'm the one best equipped to fight them. I can stay underwater a mighty long time."

"How long?" my grandfather asks.

Ed shrugs. "Never been tested."

"At least six minutes," I offer, recalling the time I timed him, though I know from our adventures on the Black Sea he can handle being submerged for longer.

Ed offers me a tiny smile. "I'll do whatever I need to— swim into that lake and learn how she's makin' them, destroy the operation, kill as many as I can, but I canna fly myself there and I donna know where it is. If ye can get me there, I'll fight them."

The dogs by the fireplace lumber to their feet. They seem to have caught the note of challenge in Ed's voice, the call to action that makes my heart hammer with a mixture of awe at Ed's bravery (he of all people knows the danger of the foes he'll be facing) and fear for his safety.

Ed tosses the halves of the bread roll to the dogs, and they catch them from the air, swallowing them down.

My mother has been mostly silent through this discussion. Now she sighs. "We fought Eudora off long ago. Since then, I've only been focused on keeping my children safe. We've holed up in this fortress, even fled to the states, all in an effort to keep them out of her reach. But she's not content to stay away, is she? We can't hide away forever. It's time we stand and fight."

For the next hour at least, as we munch the meat cookies my mother made for dessert (meat cookies are like hamburgers, mostly, but without buns or pickles or other distractions, though we sometimes top them with cheese like you might frost a cookie, or mix in chopped mushroom or onion like real cookies have chocolate chips) we discuss logistics. My father pulls out maps, and supplies us with images his spies have sent him—pictures and even video footage, most of it grainy and distant, of whatever Eudora is up to at the lake.

We don't have a great deal of intel on what's going on up in Siberia. True, my father has spies up there, but he doesn't get phone calls or e-mails from them any more than he does from my mother, and for the same reason. It would be too easy for Eudora to hack into the transmission and find out everything he knows, along with the identities of his spies. We can't risk that.

So the spies mostly keep watch and occasionally visit us with information. They exist mostly to keep us safe, and in the case of my grandmother, they alerted my grandfather to the fact that there was another dragon on the earth.

And it's not just Eudora they're spying on.

There's another dragon in Siberia, living near Eudora, who in some ways is even more dangerous than Eudora, because he's still a dragon. His name is Ion and my father absolutely hates him, on account of the last time they fought, Ion very nearly killed him by tearing open his softer underbelly with his horns (remember, our scales are armored to resist nearly anything—bullets, swords, fire—but our slightly-softer underbellies can be pierced by another dragon's horns or talons or even tail spikes).

Ion lives in a castle near Eudora and has been known to work with her. My dad's spies keep watch over both of them, but the spies have reported that they sometimes suspect Ion knows what they're up to, spying on him. We're not sure if this is pure paranoia on their part or if there really is something to it. Ion did live among us, for a time, long ago, though he was most likely acting as a double agent, spying on behalf of Eudora while trying to make my grandfather and father believe he was on their side.

And by the same token, it's entirely possible that Ion and Eudora have spies among us—villagers they befriended while Ion lived here, who still feel enough sympathy or allegiance to him that they'd keep him informed of what we're up to.

For that reason, we've got to keep all our plans quiet, and make our moves with stealth. Even though everyone's eager to be part of Ed's raiding party, we can't leave the village undefended. Some of us have got to stay behind and help cover for those who've gone.

My brothers both want to go, on account of neither of them have met the enemy and they both think they need the experience. My parents want to go, too, since they've fought the regular yagi the most, and even faced Eudora, so they know a bit more about what they're doing. Also, though they don't say it in as many words, I'm pretty sure they want to come along to look after their kids and make sure none of us gets hurt.

"You three girls need to stay home," my mother insists. "It's going to be dangerous, and there's no need for you to come."

Her words send a spark of anger shooting through me so strong and fast I'm tempted to stand up or stomp away in fury. "It's not too dangerous for Ram and Felix." Somehow I keep my voice level, although I want to scream.

"Wren." My mom pats my hand. "We need you to stay safe. The dragon world needs you."

"They need my womb, you mean." Okay, maybe now I am shouting just a teeny tiny bit. "*This*, mother, this is precisely why I don't want to marry. You used to be a butcher. You used to fight yagi and do brave things, but then you had dragon babies and you all but retreated back into the womb with them. I am a dragon. I have wings. I'm meant to fly, not cower in fear while someone else fights my battle for me. The water yagi attacked *me*. I have more experience with them than anyone. I need to go."

No one says a word, not even my mother.

Then my grandfather clears his throat and volunteers to stay behind. "I've fought Eudora enough times. I don't care to see her face ever again, thank you. Not that I'm afraid of her, mind you—but if everyone else wants to go, I don't mind staying home."

"Thank you, Father," Mom says without looking at me. "But we have two villages to protect, so we'll need more than one dragon to stay behind. Is it too much to assume that my other daughters care enough about the continuation of the species to tend the hearth while we're gone?"

Rilla raises her hands in a gesture of innocence. "I'm cool. I'll stay. Siberia holds no allure for me."

But beside her, across the table from me, Zilpha's neck is flaming red like she sometimes gets when she's nervous or embarrassed, and she's making a tortured face.

"Zilpha?" My mom only says her name, but there's so much in that word. It's more than just a question, asking if she's okay, asking if she isn't going to stay home like her obedient sister. There's an undercurrent of *et tu, Brute*, almost as though she fears Zilpha will turn on her just as I did. And the implication that Zilpha, of all people, *Zilpha*, who's always only ever wanted to marry and make dragon babies, surely Zilpha knows it's her place to stay home.

Zilpha speaks. "I'd like to go. I can help Wren watch out for Ed."

My mouth drops open to protest that I never implied anything about my going has to do with Ed, but then my sister gives me a flickering glance with a hint of pleading, and I remember that we triplets have an unspoken agreement. We're co-conspirators. We might fight amongst ourselves, but we stand together against anyone else.

Even our mother.

And besides which, I want to hook Zilpha up with Ed. Is that what she's getting at—that she's softening to the idea after all, and only needs me to choreograph their romance? Zilpha is all about romance.

And my mom is all about finding her daughter a mate. I leap to my sister's defense and clap my hand over my mother's hand which is resting near mine on the table. "That's right, Mom. I need Zilpha to come, too, so we can be there for Ed."

The hand-grabbing did the trick, getting her to look at me in surprise just long enough for me to flash her a big wink, my body turned with my back to Ed so he doesn't see. Maybe our seating arrangement isn't so bad, after all.

And my mom stammers her startled agreement, though she looks slightly confused afterward about why, exactly, she agreed.

With that much decided, my father announces that we should all retire for the evening (it is getting quite late) and think on our plans, then gather again tomorrow to sort out more details.

I was exhausted before we sat down to eat. As the excitement of our discussion ebbs rapidly away, I feel almost as though I could fall asleep in my chair. I rise and excuse myself to my room.

Ed rises, as well, and I'm about to take a moment to tell him goodnight and thank him for his bravery in volunteering to fight the monsters, but he turns away from me and talks to Felix instead.

Well enough. We've been practically glued to each other the past few days. We need to step apart, especially if he's going to start a romance with my sister.

I help clear the table, then head down the long stone corridor that cuts through the mountain to the bedrooms. But before I reach my room, I hear Zilpha's voice, speaking softly, audible to my ears only because of the acoustics of the stone walls.

"Ed? Can I talk to you?"

I force myself to walk a few more steps, casually, as though I haven't heard. But on the inside I'm doing something like a victory dance. Zilpha wants to talk to Ed! This is a great sign. This is wonderful.

"Aye. What's on yer mind?"

"Let's talk in the study."

I give them another couple of seconds to duck into the study, which I passed many steps ago. Then I slip off my sandals and tiptoe back after them. The corridor is dark and empty. The rest of my family has lingered in the dining room or is helping my mom in the kitchen, cleaning up after the big meal. I'd have stuck around to help more, but I'm likely to drop the dishes in my exhaustion and I'd probably just be in the way.

But I'm not too tired to listen to whatever's about to pass between Ed and Zilpha. Maybe eavesdropping doesn't seem like the nicest thing I could be doing, but if it's going to help me get those two together, I'm going to do it.

Dragon posterity may well depend on it.

Besides, it will save Zilpha recounting the conversation, later. As of the glance she gave me at dinner, we're co-conspirators. She'd want me to listen in. Maybe she even caught up to Ed while I was in the hallway precisely so I could still hear them and would know to circle back. We triplets can be very sneaky that way.

I reach the doorway and hang back, just out of sight, as my sister's words float softly through the open doors.

Chapter Seventeen

"She didn't mean it that way."

For a second, I'm not sure what Zilpha's talking about. Obviously I've missed something. Ed and Zilpha have had a moment to talk while I was approaching at a tiptoe, and I've picked up the conversation partway through.

Ed's voice sounds almost mournful, "Aye, she did. 'Twas a message meant clearly for me, and I shoulda picked up on it sooner without her havin' to spell it out in front of everyone. She's a dragon. She can fly. She willna hide while others fight. It's more than that she doesna care for me. I disgust her."

I'm clenching the wall to keep myself from bursting in and explaining that I didn't mean those words as a message to Ed. In fact, so far was that idea from my mind, that even as Ed repeats my speech verbatim, it takes me a moment of deep denial before I realize I said that. He's talking about me.

And he thinks I was talking about him.

Of course he does. He can't fly. And when the dragon hunters of old attacked Nattertinny Castle and killed his parents, Ed hid. He hid because his parents told him to—because he'd be dead if he didn't. But even though I'm glad he hid (because otherwise I'd never have met him, and what a loss that would be) he feels guilty about hiding. He feels guilty that he's alive and they're dead—so guilty, that even though I didn't mean to, I struck that tender nerve with a precision that smacks of betrayal.

I suck. I am a bad, bad, bad friend.

Worst ever.

I am not even worthy to be Ed's friend.

I step away and continue on down the corridor, forcing myself to head to my bedroom instead of turning around and explaining myself, or listening to hear more.

I've heard enough. And painful though it feels to think Ed thinks I think that, I don't know what I could say to him to make him understand I truly don't. But more than that, most importantly of all, really, it's probably better this way. I would never intentionally say anything so cutting, but now that it's said and I don't know how to take it back, maybe it's for the best.

Ed needs to fall in love with Zilpha. What better way for that to happen, than for him to think I'm disgusted by him? He can turn to Zilpha for comfort and reassurance. It will grow into love from there.

It's bound to. Zilpha specifically requested to come along to Siberia, not because she wants to fight water yagi or visit Siberia, but to get to know Ed. She's on board with the plan. And this is a good way, maybe even the best way, to get Ed turned away from me and aligned to her.

I reach my room, peel off my dress, and tug on a nightshirt. It's burning inside me, the guilt of what I said, the pain in Ed's voice, the desire to run back and correct them both. But if I did that, it would only be for me, to restore myself in his esteem.

But for the sake of the romance that needs to blossom between him and Zilpha, I can't do that.

I curl into a ball in my bed, clutching the pillow I abandoned only hours ago, suffocating my tears in its softness. I hate crying. Really, a despise it. I'm a dragon, mighty and strong and fearless, and I am not in love with Ed. I was *never* in love with Ed.

So why does his pain cut into my heart?
*

The next morning I'm reluctant to get up and join the others at breakfast because I don't want to face Ed. But at the same time, I need to see if anything's happening with him and Zilpha. Considering what I've let him believe of me, the two of them ought to be all but engaged by now.

But I find only my brothers at the table. My mom is puttering in the kitchen. Speaking of people holding a grudge against me, she gives me the stink eye as I enter.

143

I muster an innocent smile. "What is there for breakfast? Eggs?"

"Or leftovers from last evening." She extends her coffee mug in the direction of the fridge.

I pull a leg of lamb, untouched and still on the bone, from the fridge, and blow a light stream of fire over it to warm it.

"Mind the air," my mom says, flipping on the exhaust hood over the range. "We don't want the whole house to reek of mutton."

I obediently position myself next to the range, holding the lamb under the hood as I heat it with my breath, grateful for the noise which means I don't have to talk to my mother, who looks to be in a sour mood.

But eventually the meat is heated through, and I have no choice but to switch off the hood and face her. "Any more of that coffee?"

She nods to the pot. "Help yourself."

I've got my hands full with the lamb and she's standing there doing nothing. "You can't pour me a cup?"

"I'm sorry?" My mom snaps. "I thought you were so bloody autonomous. Or do you need me to wait on you as a means of keeping me in my place?"

"What?" I pull a mug out of the cupboard. I'm not sure I want her to pour me coffee in this mood—she might splash it on me when she hands it over. "What are you talking about?" I'm a little groggy yet, on account of I haven't had my coffee, otherwise I might have gathered sooner what she was steamed about.

"I'm a mother, tantamount to servant. I have given the last twenty plus years to you children and you despise me for it."

I study her over my coffee as I take my first sip of the morning, and I realize what she's saying. It's the same speech that upset Ed. For a moment I sip my coffee, choosing my words carefully. They've gotten me into enough trouble lately. I want to make this better, not worse. So I pull from the angle she's bound to find most sympathetic.

144

"You've asked me, I don't know how many times, why I don't want to marry. And then the closest I come to telling you my heartfelt answer, you get upset. This is why I can't tell you."

Mom gives me a look that might as well have fire shooting from it. "You don't want to marry and become a mother, because you don't want to end up like me."

I hadn't thought about it in those terms, but now that she's said it, I realize it's precisely true. My mother, in all the stories my father and grandfather have told, used to be this amazing dragon, and a butcher, fierce with her swords. She turned Eudora into only human. She used to shoot flaming arrows and fight off yagi by the score. She was brave and strong and powerful and feared.

And now she bakes dinner rolls no one wants to eat. It's a tad pathetic.

It's true. I don't want to end up like her.

And now her voice is this pained whisper of pleading. "You're not going to deny it?"

By rights, I know I should deny it, but I'm too stunned to speak. It's like she's held up a mirror to my face and shown me my true feelings, my true fears. I don't want to marry, because I don't want to end up like my mother.

I open my mouth, too late, to say something, even though I don't know what to say, but she's already spun around and left the room. I follow her through the door to the dining room even as she heads down the hallway. I'm carrying my coffee in one hand and leg of lamb in the other, and my mom has a strong rule about food not going out of the dining room to the rest of the house, so I let her go and I sit at the table with my brothers.

"Anyone else hate me today?" I ask, tearing into my meat without looking at them. They've got to have overheard my entire conversation with my mother. The dining room is open to the kitchen, and everything echoes.

They're silent for a bit, then Felix laughs. "It's times like this I wonder why I want to find a dragon woman to marry."

But Ram only scowls at him. "The womb is stronger than the sword," he says cryptically, in his usual stoic fashion. Then he stands to leave.

Since I don't know what he's getting at and I don't really believe him, I ask, "What do you mean?"

"The sword can only take life. The womb can grant it." He gives me the kind of level, solemn look that makes him seem so much older than a single year my senior. He steps toward the corridor, then pauses. "Empires rise, not on the strength of their armies, but at the breasts of their mothers."

I stare after him after he's left, thinking on what he's said. I've always venerated the sword and resented the womb, so my instinct is to disregard his words and deny their truth. But I can't think of a solid argument against them.

Fortunately Felix is incapable of being serious. No sooner has the sound of Ram's footsteps died away down the hall, than our little brother guffaws heartily. "Ram said breast!"

Tempted as I am to chide him for being juvenile, I decide to use my mouth for eating instead of talking. I've made enough people angry with me, and we need to work as a team if we're going to defeat the water yagi. I'd best not upset anyone else.

*

Since it's been decided my grandfather and Rilla will stay in Azerbaijan, my grandfather has returned to his village while the rest of us make our plans. We've got to keep our plans under wraps in case Ion or Eudora have spies in the village.

The rest of us gather standing around the dining room table which is spread, not with food this time, but with maps. Ed has taken a post between my brothers. He only glances my way briefly, and then gives me a tight-lipped smile. Gone is the friendly demeanor I've grown so accustomed to over the last few days.

If I hadn't overheard his words to my sister last night, I might have attributed his attitude to the seriousness of our plans. But I know better.

146

The look he gives me is almost identical to the one my mother flashes my way, her eyes tinged with a disappointment akin to grief. I wish I knew what to say to raise her spirits, but other than deny the truth of everything that passed between us this morning, I can't think of anything. And she wouldn't believe me if I denied those words, especially since I still believe them true.

So I focus on the plans, because none of the difficulties between me and my mother or me and Ed will matter if we don't pull off this mission. There's danger in those waters, as my father reminds us many times while he spells out our strategy.

"The lake lies three miles due south of Eudora's fortress, which is east of Ion's castle." He marks each on the map in turn as he speaks of them, three red dots marking the points of a triangle. "Our spies live here, in a cabin, about halfway between Ion's castle and the lake. We'll stay with our spies. They don't know we're coming, so we'll stop short, in these woods, here, and I'll go first, with Felix, so we don't overwhelm them. Then, if it's clear for you to join us, Felix will return to bring the rest of you to the spy house. From there, I'd like to visit the lake, but we'll proceed according to the advice of our spies."

As he talks, I'm studying the map. Siberia isn't familiar to me at all, and while I intend to stick close to my party, I still want to know where I'm headed.

We'll be far north, east of the Lena River, in a remote mountainous region of boreal forest. There will be woods and mountains to help hide us, which should be helpful. "Where are the roads and towns?" I ask, leaning over the map of the larger region.

My father meets my eyes. "There are a few dirt roads, a few small settlements, some abandoned prisoner of war camps, but mostly there is wide open country, brutal in winter, impassible in rain, inaccessible to many except by air."

"The perfect place for a dragon to hide," someone whispers, the voice so soft I can't identify who spoke.

"Don't they wonder what our spies are doing out there?" Zilpha asks. "Don't they stand out?"

"The region is primarily Turkic in ethnicity," my father explains, "but even still, Xalil is there by Ion's invitation."

"What?" Felix sounds as shocked as I feel. "Ion invited Xalil to spy on him?"

My father looks at Felix with his usual long-suffering patience. "As you may recall, in years past, before any of you were born, in the years while your mother was away at boarding school in England, Ion lived in your grandfather Elmir's village. We were wary of him. He was an outsider. We didn't trust him, but since he was a dragon, we let him live among us in light of his story that he was alone in the world and only wanted to be among his own kind.

"But he betrayed that trust and tried to kidnap your mother. Following that attempt, he teamed up with Eudora to attack our village, all-but-killing me in the process. He has never attempted to return, but fled to his castle in the mountains near Eudora.

"During his time among us, Ion had befriended Xalil. In fact, Xalil is a," my father makes a face, thinking, "not a chiropractor, not properly. But more than a message therapist. I suppose you could call him a musculoskeletal practitioner. Whatever his title, Xalil had worked with Ion while he lived among us, and Ion invited him to come to Siberia and work with him there."

"Ion has his own musculoskeletal practitioner on retainer?" Zilpha asks, with only the tiniest bit of jealousy in her voice.

Ed grunts in agreement. "I could use one of those."

I smile and keep my mouth shut, even though, frankly, I'd like a good chiropractic massage, too. Zilpha and Ed have something in common. It's a step in the right direction, even if it's something everyone in the room also agrees with.

My father shrugs. "Ion suffers from some sort of ailment and the cold makes it worse. I'm not sure what it is, nor does it matter. The point is, when Xalil received Ion's invitation, he came to Elmir and asked what to do. They agreed it would be helpful to have a spy in the area, since the spies who'd watched over Eudora's household in previous years were growing old and were no longer up to the task. But to avoid rousing any suspicion, Xalil told Ion that part of his reason for agreeing to move to Siberia, was because he felt his neighbors disapproved of his previous associations with Ion."

Zilpha clarifies, "So, Xalil made it sound like he wasn't welcome here anymore, in order to make Ion think he wouldn't report back any news?"

"Yes." My father nods. "It seems to have worked. However, Xalil is now also starting to get old. Since he's not sure how much longer he'll be up to working, his granddaughter, Jala, has joined him as an understudy of sorts, working alongside him for now, learning to take over his job when the time comes."

"Jala," Zilpha repeats the name, which I also recognize. "Was she our friend, the daughter of mom's friend Anika?"

"That's right." My mom looks surprised that we remember. "When you were very little, I used to go to your grandfather's village to see my friend. You played with her kids. Jala was one of them. But as we grew older and busier with our children, and I made more friends in this village, it was harder for me to justify making the trip, so you haven't seen Jala in over a decade."

I'm listening with only half an ear, mostly feeling impatient with Zilpha's line of questioning, because even though I vaguely remember Jala and we're going to see her again once we get there, what I mostly care about is figuring out how we're going to defeat the water yagi. As one of only two dragons present who's fought them, I rather wonder if the others perhaps underestimate the fearsomeness of the creatures.

"So," I cut in, "what's the *plan*?"

149

Chapter Eighteen

My father gives me that same patient look he gave Felix. "We'll travel to the spy house and I'll make contact with Xalil and Jala. How we proceed from there will depend largely on what we learn from them. I think we should leave as soon as we can. The sooner we put a stop to Eudora's water yagi production, the fewer water yagi we'll have to contend with. And it would be wise to travel now, while the proportions of night and day are favorable. Eudora lives at a latitude that's further north than all of Scotland. In another month, we won't get much darkness at night. We need darkness to hide us as we travel there."

"But don't we need a more specific strategy?" I ask. "How are we going to defeat the water yagi and destroy the breeding operation?"

"I don't know," my father admits. "We'll make those decisions once we get there."

Felix comes to my defense, making me glad I didn't pick a fight with him earlier, "I think what Wren may be asking, is how are we going to prepare for this? What weapons are we going to bring?"

"Weapons?" My father's been leaning over the maps on the table, and now stands upright, turning toward the door. "Follow me."

While my father's lack of strategy is less than reassuring, nonetheless, the promise of weapons makes me grin. We turn to follow him, and I fall into step next to Ed. He sees my big smile and raises an eyebrow.

"Weapons, eh?" he whispers.

"Yes." I'm still smiling at the thought of them, and relieved that Ed's still speaking to me. "We don't just hoard treasure. We've got an armory, as well."

My dad leads the way to the study, which is tucked back from the central corridor, deeper in the mountain than most of the other rooms of the house. But deeper still, behind the study's fireplace, which my father swings wide with a practiced twist of a not-solely-ornamental griffin figure on the mantel, is a tunnel that leads back, through another security door, to our armory, a cavern whose natural ceiling curves fifty feet above us.

Don't picture modern weapons. Granted, we've got a few guns, but they're mostly useless against the kinds of enemies we fight. The majority of the weapons in the armory are swords of various lengths and curvatures, along with their sheaths and scabbards. We also have a fantastic selection of daggers, and enough bows, longbows, compound bows, and crossbows, to outfit the entire family four times over.

Beyond that, it's just the usual odd assortment of spears and javelins, battle axes, slingshots, catapults, and canon housed behind locked glass doors in a cavernous chamber carved from the rock. Long before my father's village was built or our fortress home even imagined, my dad's ancestors holed up in this cave in the mountain with their treasure hoard and their weapons. Some of each of those are with us still. Fluorescent lights fill the sconces where long ago, torches would have burned to light the room.

We spend the rest of the morning suiting ourselves up, strapping daggers to our thighs, fitting double baldrics across our backs and adjusting the straps until we can pull swords simultaneously from both shoulders. My mom taught us the move years ago when she trained us to fight, but we've rarely had to use it on real yagi. On those rare occasions when our mutant enemies attacked us during our travels, my parents handled the bulk of the fighting, protecting us kids, who only had to decapitate a stray yagi or two. We've never had to defend ourselves against possible hordes of them.

Until now.

Of course, even as we're outfitting ourselves for battle, I can't help thinking, time and again, that few of these weapons will do us any good. And I try to warn my family members.

"It's going to be difficult to use swords underwater," I remind them. "The weight of all these weapons would pull us down. We'll drown ourselves without any help from the water yagi."

"I'm not going in the water with all my swords on," Felix assures me. "But I want them with me if I need them. We'll be close to Eudora's fortress, you know. There will be land yagi afoot, besides just water yagi."

I know he's not refuting my warning to be mean, and he makes a valid point, but on top of everything else today—angering my mother without meaning to, and the distance Ed has been keeping from me—I feel like I've been pushed down, tugged under some invisible lake by yet another grasping hand. My lungs squeeze in response, even while I try to convince myself it's nothing.

But then a familiar Scottish brogue joins the conversation. "What yer sister's tryin' to tell ye, is that fightin' water yagi is different from fightin' the land beasties. The tricks ye know and the skills yer mother's given ye are as likely to cause ye trouble as save ye from it. Might be Wren could show ye how she killed 'em, seein' that she and I are the only ones here who've ever met the devils, and she slew a far cry more than I did."

Appreciation wells inside me as my siblings turn to me for instruction. I glance toward Ed, intending to give him a look of gratitude, but he turns his head away before I can even meet his eyes.

He still feels rejected by me.

And yet, he's taken my side in front of my siblings.

There's no time to worry about it or even feel guilty. I grab one of the patched and tattered yagi dummies from a bin, the straw-stuffed targets we used to practice with in years past, and I explain my technique.

"It's mighty hard to strike with accuracy underwater, and the resistance against your blade will exhaust your muscles in a fraction of the time of fighting in air. Instead, what I found worked best was to fly low, pluck a yagi or two from the seething swarm, and toss them high in the sky."

To demonstrate, I throw the dummy toward the distant ceiling of the cave. My siblings stand far back from me as I leap into the air in human form to simulate flight, and swing at the dummy as it falls.

"You can decapitate them in the air far easier than underwater, without getting close enough for them to mob you." I survey my siblings, awaiting their response.

Ram crosses to the bin of dummies and tosses one in the air, sending straw showering down on us as he leaps and slices off its head.

Within minutes, all of my siblings are doing the same.

I duck away toward the hall that leads to the study. In the midst of the flying straw, I don't notice Ed headed the same direction until he joins me in the shelter of the doorway.

"Thank you," I tell him sincerely, trying to meet his eyes.

"I did nothin'." Ed watches my siblings instead of looking at me.

"You did," I insist. "And I appreciate it."

Ed's still facing the others, but with his sharp goatee, I can see so much more of his face than ever before, and like all dragons, he can communicate effectively with his features, even if he doesn't intend to. Right now, the way he swallows, pinches his lips, and blinks rapidly, the message is a complicated one, but still reasonably clear.

He feels hurt by what I said last night. He doesn't want to talk about it, doesn't even believe that my thanks are sincere, since he doesn't think I respect him.

There might be more than that there, but I can't look any longer. I stare at the natural stone cave floor, which is quickly becoming covered by straw from the beheaded yagi dummies.

Later, once everyone has grown tired of the exercise and feels secure with their weapons and left the room to find lunch, I sweep up the straw and shove it back inside the bodies, and grab the mending kit to patch the heads back on. We never bother with very many stitches, since the dummies are only going to get beheaded again.

I've got half the pile finished when I hear footsteps approaching from down the hall.

I feel a twinge of disappointment when I see who it is, even though I should have known by the rhythm of the footsteps. It's my mom. She's brought me lunch.

"Thanks. My hands are full. You can just set it there."

"Thank you for cleaning up the armory. Usually I have to do it." She sighs.

I stab the needle through the rough fabric. Maybe I should say something, but when I try out the words in my head, no matter how I intend them, I still hear her taking them in a defensive way. And what was it she always told us? If you can't say anything nice, don't say anything at all.

So after a few moments of silence, I simply say, "Thanks again for bringing me lunch."

And she leaves.

Maybe I didn't make it better, but at least I didn't make it worse.

Not much worse, anyway.

*

We depart at nightfall. Maybe that seems soon, but over supper we all agreed there's nothing to be gained by waiting. We need to know what we're up against, which means checking out the lake and learning all we can about how Eudora's churning out the water yagi. It could take us days or even weeks to gather the information we need once we get up there.

So there's no sense waiting around.

My father and brothers take turns hauling Ed on their backs. Even with a bit of breeze more or less in their favor, each of them is eager to hand him off at the end of the two-hour shifts. And in the morning, as we're making camp in a remote stretch of Russia north of Kazakhstan, my father shakes his head at me. "I don't know how you hauled him all the way home from Scotland."

I smile. "That's why it took me so long to get home—that, and fighting the water yagi."

To my relief, the day is uneventful. I sleep nearly fourteen hours straight. I may not have hauled a hydra on my back, but it's still exhausting flying so far, and I'm not fully recovered from my previous journey. We flew fairly fast, too, more north than east, on account of the direction of the wind. It was a gamble, taking what we could get and using it to our best advantage, hoping we'd have a more easterly wind to push us to our destination the next night.

But we rise to a stiff breeze punching us back from the east, trying to push us west. We're still less than halfway to our destination (we may have made it to Russia already, but it's a very big country—the biggest on earth—especially west to east), so I know we won't reach the spy cabin by morning. I checked the map on my tablet and the trip would take over eighty hours by car (and that's just the driving, not even factoring in sleep), so I'm glad we're flying and don't have to follow the circuitous mountain roads.

In fact, we're purposely avoiding roads, towns, and anywhere else where people might spot us flying overhead. To avoid drawing attention to ourselves, we keep our glow at its dimmest and spread out in the sky, to the point where each of us can only see the two or three dragons nearest them at any time. And we fly low, out of range of radar detection.

The closer we get to Eudora's fortress, the less careful we have to be of humans, there being far fewer of them, and the more cautious we have to be about Eudora, the yagi, and any other potential spies she might have posted about.

155

We fly until dawn. The wind lets up a bit toward morning, but we're still beat by the time we make camp, and we didn't make near the progress we'd hoped for. The only good thing about being so exhausted, is that there's little time for conversation (normally I enjoy chatting, but right now, with Ed and my mom both feeling sorely towards me, I'd rather avoid it).

My father, who led the way most of the night, except for the stretch of the trip when he carried Ed, lands first. After my mom joins him on the ground, he sets off in search of supper.

By the time the rest of us have landed and drunk our fill from a nearby stream, my dad's back, arriving in dragon form with a whole elk dangling from each foot.

We eat, our mouths too busy tearing meat to speak. And then we shuffle about, each of us picking a spot to settle down to sleep. The woods are typical of northern latitudes—lots of trees, mostly evergreen, with little growing between them on account of the brutal winters that cover the ground with snow for so many months out of the year, and the pine needles that cloak the forest floor. There are some bushes and smaller plants, but it's not a tangle like Azerbaijan's subtropical forests.

I'm scoping out a spot for my bed when I realize Zilpha has slipped away. We're on a high plateau-like ridge in the mountains, a flat-ish cleft overlooking a valley, with stunning peaks rising up around us. The view is magnificent, and sure enough, Zilpha's perched on a jutting granite boulder, watching the sunrise streak the sky with glorious shades of magenta and crimson.

Hoping to gauge her feelings to learn if she's growing fond of Ed, and also just to check on her and make sure she's okay and not secretly mad at me, too, I head over and join her on the rock (it's a very big rock).

I don't say anything.

Zilpha glances at me, gives me a look of acknowledgement that's not really a smile but is still welcoming, and turns back to watching the sky. After a while, she says, "It's beautiful, isn't it?"

"Sure is. Kind of reminds me of Montana." The school we go to in the states is in Montana, a place we picked for several reasons. The mountains remind us of home. The region isn't densely populated, which means we can occasionally fly as dragons without so much risk of being seen. And unlike some of the more southerly regions of the Rocky Mountains, there isn't nearly as much flyover traffic in Montana as there is in Utah (all those people going to Phoenix and LA, I guess). Minimal flyover traffic is important for the same reason as sparse population—if we want to come and go as dragons, we need to stay out of sight.

So we're drawn to remote areas like this one.

Zilpha muses, "I always thought of Siberia as being desolate, but this is beautiful. It's a wonder more people don't live here."

"The winters are crazy harsh, I guess. And it's mega remote, you know. If you can't fly in like we do, it would take days and days to get here."

"But it's the perfect place for a dragon to live."

I can't help laughing at the accuracy of her statement. "Too bad Eudora figured that out first."

"I wonder if there are any others."

"Dragons?"

"Dragons," my sister affirms. "Living in the mountains out here. Maybe that's part of what keeps people away, you know? Myths of fire-breathing creatures, wild country, harsh winters."

"Well, Ion lives out here, too." I name the other arch-enemy of our family, the dragon who nearly killed my father a little over two decades ago.

But at the same time, I sense what she's getting at. Zilpha has been searching for a husband for years, even before she was old enough to marry, hoping to have one picked out and ready to go before she even needed him. She feels impatient that she hasn't found one yet.

She sighs wistfully. "In the stories, you always hear of dragons living in mountain caves."

157

"The altitude helps us take flight easily," I acknowledge, not quite comfortable with the direction this conversation is taking, trying to steer her to something practical. I like to speculate about the possibility of other dragons as much as anyone, but does my sister really think there might be another dragon out there, somewhere among the endless mountain peaks? Why does she care anymore? She doesn't need to find one, not if she's got Ed.

Unless she has no intention of marrying Ed.

Chapter Nineteen

My pulse quickens with something akin to dread. Why is Zilpha talking about this? Doesn't she like Ed? Why would she reject him? It would hurt his feelings even more on top of the way I've let him think I don't care for him…and how can she reject him, after I've let him think that about me specifically so he'd draw closer to her?

In spite of my efforts to steer the conversation away from the topic of other dragons, Zilpha is undeterred. "I wish there was some signal we could transmit to send a message if there's another dragon out there—that we're here, we're friendly, and we're looking for them."

"That's one of the difficulties we have as a species. It's hard to find each other when we're all in hiding." I pause, thinking, then continue. "Still, don't you think that's something our spies would know about? That's what they're up here doing, right? Keeping an eye on dragons? If there's more than Ion and Eudora out here, they'd have some idea."

"I'll talk to Jala tomorrow." Zilpha agrees readily.

It's been burning in my gut through the whole conversation, and given how strongly Zilpha has stuck to the idea of finding another dragon, I can't walk away without knowing why she's so determined when she doesn't need to be. "Why do you want to find another dragon?"

She whips her head around, meeting my eyes for the first time since I joined her on the rock. "I need a mate."

"What's wrong with Ed?"

Zilpha makes a condescending sound in her throat. "Seriously?"

"Yes, seriously. What's wrong with him?" My face may be a bit flushed right now, but let's blame that on the rosy light of dawn. I know Ed has some minor deformities and can't fly and all, but he's fun and sweet and considerate and strong and handsome and hunky. And he has amazing skills in the water. Besides all that, he's the Loch Ness Monster. He's legendary.

"He's a brute," Zilpha answers back. "He's not sophisticated or cosmopolitan or romantic. He's none of the things I've ever dreamed about in a husband. I want a guy who can serenade me. I bet Ed can't even play an instrument with his hands the way they are. I've been dreaming of a husband all my life. I picture a man who's cultured, who knows about history and politics and people, who can have fascinating conversations. A guy who can cook various cuisines, who travels to exotic destinations and can speak multiple languages. Ed can barely speak English."

"He's perfectly literate. He just has an accent. The man's like 600 years old. He has an old Scottish accent. You make him sound like he's some kind of caveman." I've always known my sister was a romantic at heart, that she had a vision of what she wanted in a husband—a lofty vision few real guys could ever fit. And she'll never find a dragon like that, so she might as well abandon the idea.

"He *is* some kind of caveman. He's been holed up in that castle, in that lake, for centuries," Zilpha insists. "I know I seem like I'm desperate to marry, but I'm not *that* desperate. I have fire inside me. Ed's like cold water. I've thought about it, Wren, but I just can't. Cold water on fire? He'd douse me."

"You'd rather risk being single forever than marry Ed?" I'm aghast. Personally, I don't see anything wrong with hiding out at Nattertinny Castle for centuries. Especially if Ed is there. And I don't think of him as cold water at all—and I'm the one who's afraid of water, or at least deep water. I'm the hydrophobic.

"There's got to be another dragon out there." Zilpha studies the horizon, now fully lit by the dawn.

"You don't know that there is. Maybe Ed's your only option."

"I'm going to live a long time." Zilpha unfolds her legs from their seated position and prepares to stand. "I'll take my chances."

I stand, too, ready to be done with this conversation before I say something to make yet another family member angry with me. I could tell her all the fantastic things Ed has going for him, but she's already demonstrated that she's made up her mind. She'll only fight me.

When I turn to head back to the camp, I see a movement among the trees. My hand falls to the hilt of the sword strapped in its scabbard to the belt at my hips, and I sniff the air for anything that might smell like yagi, but then I recognize a sheepish face as the figure steps around a clump of trees.

"I came to fetch ye. We're all bedded down for the night." Ed explains.

Zilpha darts past him toward our camp, leaving the two of us alone.

I glance at the trees Ed emerged from. Was Ed hiding, listening to us? Maybe he came upon us while we were talking, realized it was a bad time to butt in, and ducked out of sight. In my mind, I quickly I review everything Zilpha and I said. We were certainly talking loudly enough, he could have heard us from the trees—heard us distinctly enough to catch every word, actually.

And none of it would make him feel any better than my thoughtless comments two nights ago. I should really stop speaking. Ever.

Ed's standing in front of me while I sort this all through. I'm trying to think if there's anything I could say to make the situation better instead of worse.

I've got nothing.

Ed looks down at his hands. "I canna play the piano, or the bagpipes or the guitar. None of that. Me fingers aren't flexible enough." His confession sounds apologetic, with a twinge of grief.

161

I reach out and take his hands in mine. "They're good hands," I try to tell him, but my voice has gone raspy and hollow and I don't know if the words came out right. Instead of trying to speak again (it doesn't feel like I'd have any better luck on a second go) I lift his hands to my lips and kiss his knuckles.

I know, I know. This is not the way to make Ed prefer Zilpha to me. I know that. But you know what else? I don't know how to make Zilpha and Ed love each other. I'm going to keep trying, of course, but I haven't yet found the key to unlock that puzzle. I just know that Ed is hurting, and I can't walk away without trying to comfort him.

So then I stand there for who knows how long, with his hands in mine, his knuckles pressed against my lips, staring into his eyes as though I might find the answers there. Oh Ed, why can't you just fall in love with Zilpha?

And why does Zilpha care if Ed can play an instrument, or any of those things? She's a good enough pianist herself to make up for any lack of skills in her mate.

"I was hatched in 1482," Ed admits softly, "but me egg was laid three years before that, so I've never been clear on what age that makes me."

I squeeze Ed's hands. What can I say? He was hatched before Christopher Columbus sailed to America, before the vast majority of the events I ever learned about in history class even happened. "You're timeless," I whisper, my voice still gone.

But Ed only looks sad. "I'm a relic. Maybe I don't belong in this world any more than a caveman."

He starts to pull away, to walk away, but I squeeze his fingers and pull him back, "All dragons are relics. My grandmother Faye didn't think she belonged in this world either, remember?"

Ed hangs his head and lets go of my hands. As he's turning to leave, in a brogue made thick by emotion, he says, "Maybe she was right." And he walks away.

162

Given his heavy accent, I have to sort out the words after he speaks them, so it doesn't even register what he's said until he's a few steps ahead of me on the way back to the camp. I stand there, stunned, a moment longer. How can Ed think that?

I follow him back to camp, but he's already bedded down on the other side of my sleeping brother Ram, with some trees on the other side of him, so there's no room for me. I could walk over there, but I'd risk waking and upsetting my brother. And I don't know what I'd say anyway, so I leave it at that.

Still, it troubles me as I make my own bed of pine needles and stretch out with my cloak draped over me (did I explain to you about the cloaks? We carry them in our backpacks when we travel in colder climates. They don't get shredded, either, if we have to change into dragon form unexpectedly). I'm still thinking about it as I try to fall asleep, but I don't have the answer.

I mean, I know we may be relics, but we still have a place in this world. We've fought to keep that place, and we're trying to find mates so we can continue on for another generation. I know we deserve to exist.

I'm just not sure why.

*

I wake up thinking maybe my mom would know the answer, or at least know how my grandma Faye got over thinking she didn't belong in this world. But then I remember that my mom is mad at me for saying I don't want to be like her—which if you think about it, is a dumb reason for being mad at someone. It's not like I don't still love her. Of course I love my mom.

You can love someone or something without wanting to be like them. I love roasted elk meat, but that doesn't mean I want to *be* roasted elk meat.

So, the bad news is I don't know how to ask my mom about my grandmother's existential conundrum. But the good news is my dad has gone hunting and returned with two more elk (Zilpha is right about how awesome it would be to live here. Siberia is thick with elk. Who knew?) And I guess if I have to pick between understanding the meaning of my existence or eating roast elk, I'm going to go with the elk, at least for this morning, because after having flown all night for two nights in a row, I'm am insanely hungry, never mind that I already ate a large portion of elk for supper last night. And I can't eat and talk at the same time, not really.

So I eat.

When we're done with breakfast, we gather our things and take to the sky again. The wind is nearly still tonight. What little bit of breeze we do have is hitting us head-on, but as long as it stays gentle it's actually helpful at keeping us aloft. We're not flying as fast as we might with a tailwind, but a gentle headwind creates some of the best conditions for gliding (if you've ever flown a kite, you can visualize how this is true).

And since we don't have too much further to go, there's no need to fly hard and fast. We reach the woods near the spy house a couple hours before sunrise, and we land among the trees. As planned, my father and Felix proceed ahead of the rest of us to let the spies know what we're up to. My brother Ram and my mom go hunting, leaving me and Ed and Zilpha alone in the woods. We switch over to human form and pull our cloaks immediately from our backpacks, shivering as we wrap them around us, because the farther north we go into Siberia, the colder it gets.

I'm wary because it's still dark out and we're only about five miles from Eudora's fortress, which means there are probably yagi around somewhere, and from what we know of them, they can track dragons by scent. Because of the likelihood of encountering yagi in the area, we're all doubling up—Dad with Felix, Ram with Mom, me and Zilpha with Ed.

So then I'm trying to think how to use this time to generate something between Ed and Zilpha, but my brain is foggy from a long night of flying, and I don't know how to get them together. I've been trying for days, really, and they don't seem any closer now than the moment they first met.

Before I can think what to talk about, Ram and my mom return with a bear and a couple of musk deer. And then I'm back to the conundrum of not being able to talk because I'm eating. And before I can even finish that, Felix arrives to tell us we're clear to proceed to the spy house.

I take to the sky with mixed feelings. In some ways, I'm excited that we're closer to learning what the water yagi are, and hopefully destroying Eudora's means of producing them. But I'm also worried about the dangers Ed might have to face.

And it feels like I'm running out of time to convince Zilpha to fall in love with Ed. Maybe that's not true, maybe time is open-ended for us since we're more or less immortal, but I can't imagine Zilpha spending time with Ed once our mission is completed—especially considering that she isn't really spending time with him now, anyway.

We reach the spy house and my concerns about Ed are replaced by the uncertainties of all we still need to accomplish. The spy house is a cabin in the woods, hardly noticeable until you're upon it. We're still three miles from Eudora's fortress, and three miles from Ion's place (those two are also three miles apart from one another—all together, Ion's, Eudora's, and the spy house sort of make a triangle, or maybe more like a rectangle if you include the lake).

Dawn is nearly breaking, the eastern mountain backlit by graying sky, when we step inside the cabin. The lights are dim and the curtains drawn. We keep our voices hushed. We may be miles from Ion or Eudora, but there are sure to be yagi in the area, and there's every chance our enemies have spies watching our spies.

The light isn't much, but it's more than the star-lit sky we've been flying through, so I can see our hosts clearly. I haven't seen Xalil in years. Maybe it's because we dragons don't age at all, so the contrast is greater when we compare ourselves to humans, but he seems to have grown horribly older since last I saw him. Where once he was tall and strong, he's grown stooped and gray and feeble.

Jala, however, has grown from a child to a woman. Her mother was good friends with our mother when we were growing up, so my sisters and I were playmates with Jala even though she's four years older than we are. When we were little, we looked up to her. And while our age difference might not be so noticeable now that she's twenty-four and we're almost twenty, we still respect her as an authority on the local area, even though we're royal dragons and she's a human villager. Also, dragons tend to treat most people with respect, regardless of age or station or any of those human classifications, because that's the way we are.

Jala speaks to us now as her grandfather brews tea.

"You've arrived at a critical time. We have been discussing whether we should attempt to send you a message or travel to see you, but we were reluctant to leave the area. The lake we'd mentioned previously, the one Eudora has been visiting, is teeming with the sea creatures we told you about."

"Sea creatures?" Ram repeats.

At the same time, my mother clarifies, *"teeming?"*

And my father asks, "Can you describe the creatures to us?"

His question may sound elementary, but from what I know of my dad, I'm pretty sure he wants to learn as much as he can of what the spies have observed of the water yagi, before he colors their perception with his own observations. We don't want to assume too much.

"They remind us of yagi," Jala explains. "We've never been able to study one up close. They live in the lake, and their numbers are swelling. At times, the lake's surface appears lumpy, rippling with the heads and backs of all these creatures swarming over one another. Eudora mostly visits the lake at night, which makes it very difficult to see what she's up to, but we have footage of events which—" Jala pauses as her grandfather hands cups of tea to his visitors. Then she sighs, "I suppose, rather than try to describe it, I'll let you watch the footage yourselves."

Jala turns to a widescreen monitor and pulls up the file she's looking for. "I apologize for the dark images. It was night. Even with light-sensitive equipment, this was the best we could do. This footage was captured over the course of several different nights, beginning about two weeks ago."

My family members and I fill the cabin's main room, which is open to the kitchen. We're sitting close together on the sofa and loveseat, with my dad standing next to Xalil in the kitchen, where he still has a good view of the monitor.

I sip my tea as a dark panorama fills the screen. The lake glitters with the reflection of stars shimmering on the roiling water. In spite of the darkness, I can see the lumpiness of the lake's surface, just as Jala described it. Beyond the lake, on the shore, I can see the outline of trees and the shadows of mountains outlined by the starry sky.

Then something streaks through the sky, a glowing something. For the first fraction of a second, it looks like a meteorite, but as it nears the camera it becomes clear what it is.

A dragon.

It's got something dangling from its legs, towed by ropes, a billowy sheet of something ephemeral, almost like a parachute. And then it swoops down toward the sea and uses the chute like a dragnet, scooping up water and teeming forms, like it's fishing.

Then it rises again and flies out of sight, beyond the horizon, the net dripping and swelling with dark shapes I can only assume are that crossbreed between roaches, mercenaries, sharks, and squid. The stuff of my nightmares.

Water yagi.

Chapter Twenty

The room explodes with questions as the footage continues to play past a splice, showing the dragon's return at a slightly different angle, as the great flying beast flies to the north end of the lake, circles round again, and disappears. Then another splice, and the dragon again emerges, scoops up another net full of water yagi, and flies away.

Jala attempts to answer as many questions as she can, hushing my family. "We saw this happen two nights before we set up the camera. These images were captured on four different nights, none of them successive nights. There was one night between the first two visits, and then two nights between each of the later three.

"The dragon appears to be transporting the creatures—we can only assume he's taking them to other lakes. Based on the fact that he returns on unsuccessive nights, I'd guess the trip is too far for him to go and return in the same night, and then he rests up from his travels in between."

"So, the dragon is a 'he'?" My father asks.

Jala looks stunned and unsure of herself, as though she's been blindsided by a sudden light. "I'd assumed it was a *he* because Eudora isn't a dragon anymore, and the rest of you all haven't been up here, have you? There isn't any other dragon in the world except the one that lives three miles from the lake. I guess I'd just assumed it's Ion."

But my mother's studying the screen and frowning. "That's not Ion."

"It's—it's not?" Jala looks embarrassed now.

"What color was he?" My mom asks. The image is a blur of light on dark, the sensitivity of the equipment enhancing the contrast between darkness and pale darkness, obscuring the color completely, making the dragon a blur of light, almost white.

Jala looks at her grandfather. "A sort of fiery yellow…"

I recall what I've been taught about Ion. He's always been described to me as being a pale green, a silvery gray green.

"Yellow-orange?" Xalil suggests.

Yellow-orange isn't that different from pale green, is it? Especially when observed in the dark of night from some distance.

Jala shakes her head. "A bright fiery yellow, tinged with orange."

"Ion is a pale gray-green," my mother notes.

"I'm sorry." Jala hangs her head. "I haven't seen him in dragon form since I was two years old, and there were many dragons in the sky that day."

"Including Eudora, who was yellow." My mother places a hand on Jala's shoulder. "It's understandable that you'd assume this dragon is Ion. I knew him far better than most."

My brother Ram clears his throat. "Is it possible he's changed color in the twenty-plus years since you've seen him, Mother?"

"Only if he's also changed shape." My mom clicks a button and freezes the image on the screen, a side shot of the dragon flying, showing the profile clearly. "Ion was slender. Tall and strong, but slender. This dragon is curvier, with rounded hips and a broader chest."

My father steps past the kitchen countertop for a closer look at the screen. "You're right," he agrees. "This isn't Ion. The head shape is wrong, as well. See the nostrils? They're further back, wider set. Ion has a narrow face. Neither has Eudora learned to change herself back into a dragon. She was a shade of yellow, but with a greenish cast, not bright or orange, and she was smaller, wirier. I've never seen this dragon before."

Felix appears to be visibly excited. "Do we have any way to tell whether this dragon is male or female?"

I understand precisely why he wants to know. If it's female, it could be a mate for Felix or Ram. If it's male, it could be a potential mate for Rilla, or even Zilpha if she continues to insist on refusing Ed.

170

And if this dragon is already married, then it could have offspring of its own, potential mates for any of us.

I turn to look at Zilpha. She's riveted to the screen, an eager, almost happy look on her face.

And my heart starts to pound uneasily.

There's another dragon in the world. It's great news, I guess. It's what we've always wanted. Except...

"Don't start making wedding plans yet," Ram cautions, reading our brother's thoughts. Then Ram puts my fears into words with a somberness that flattens even Felix's smile. "Whoever this dragon is, it's working for Eudora."

Even though I'd almost reached the same conclusion, his words still knock the wind from my lungs. The implications hit me like a rain of blows. Eudora knows another dragon. The dragon is working for Eudora. Maybe the dragon knows other dragons. Maybe there's a whole team of them working for Eudora. Maybe we're outnumbered.

And alongside those blows, I'm struck by the realization that Zilpha is still looking at the screen, watching the next scene, and the next, as the dragon swoops by on return trips. It's still the same dragon each night, but that's not what bothers me. No, Zilpha doesn't look at all bothered by Ram's observation.

Doesn't she mind that this dragon is working for Eudora? Is she seriously excited about the possibility of finding a mate besides Ed? Based on what she's said to me before, I suppose she is, but where does that leave me? If Zilpha marries some other dragon, Ed will be rejected. Ed will be available.

I could marry Ed.

At this point in my frenzied thought process, I stop watching my sister and instead turn to Ed. He's standing behind the love seat, behind my brothers, watching the scene on the screen.

But he must have noticed the movement when I turned my head toward him, because he looks my way and raises his eyebrows in that open invitation, as though asking me my thoughts.

I look down at my tea cup. It's empty.

Standing, I slip past my family members and meet Ed in the kitchen, but even as our paths cross, I realize we can't talk in the kitchen any more freely than in the living room. I step outside onto the porch and Ed follows me. The sun is up and I feel my weariness acutely, in spite of the adrenaline that's surged through my veins since we've been at the cabin.

"What do ye think?" Ed asks quietly once the door is closed behind us.

"I had wondered how the water yagi were getting to all those bodies of water. They're not all connected by rivers and oceans. They had to go over land somehow."

"Looks like he was carryin' dozens, maybe several dozen if they were not yet full grown," Ed observes.

I suppose Ed wants to know my thoughts about the mysterious other dragon, but I've got to work up to that, and I'm glad he doesn't push me. "Do you suppose that dragon is working willingly for Eudora?"

"Sure looks like it, unless she's got him enslaved or somethin', but ye'd think he'd have a chance to escape, flyin' so far like he does."

"Do you think there are more of them?"

"Dragons?"

I nod.

Ed shrugs. "By the time I hatched, most dragons lived in hidin', but me parents told of a time when it wasna always so. Granted, the Crusades were over. Much of Europe had been purged of dragons by then, and yet, me parents could recall a time when there were many, even if their numbers had dwindled. They'd meet and frolic in the sky, a rainbow of different colored dragons. I always tried to imagine it. Bein' with your family these last few days is the closest I've ever come to knowin' what that's like. Still, I can't imagine they're *all* gone. A remote place like this, yer more likely to find one, I suppose. The worry's that they're workin' for Eudora."

Ed's words remind me that he's far older than my parents, than even my grandfather. He's like a window into history, filtered through the wavy glass of Loch Ness.

"Do you really believe there are more dragons?" I ask.

Ed nods hesitantly. "It's more like a hope. Can't say as it's been a steady hope. I'd resigned myself to never seein' another of me own kind, and then ye showed me yer hand." His voice grows thick.

We're leaning against the railing of the cabin, facing the woods, neither of us looking at the other directly, though we're standing close enough our arms touch. And now I lean against Ed's arm, glad for his warmth in the cool Siberian morning. Glad that I found him in spite of the vast distances between us. Glad he's no longer alone, that I took the risk of letting him see the real me.

Ed clears his throat. "What's more likely: that all the dragons, immortal though we are, have really been purged from the earth? Or that we're just all in hidin', so afeared of findin' another Eudora, we canna even show our faces to ourselves? I'm not too shocked there's another. Just disappointed Eudora found him first."

I lean on Ed's arm and we fall into companionable silence. My thoughts are shouting too loudly for me to attempt to make conversation. I certainly can't say what I'm thinking, which is that more dragons mean more potential mates, which means Zilpha doesn't have to marry Ed, which is clearly a relief to her, but leaves me in a quandary.

I hate to think of Ed going back to the loch alone. Maybe I could try to hook him up with Rilla, but she seemed less interested in him than even Zilpha, and Rilla's always said she won't marry until she finishes her degree, no matter what, and that won't be for two more years unless she hurries through her program and graduates early.

Which leaves me.

And there's part of me that thinks it would be fabulous, living at Nattertinny castle, visiting the loch with Ed, eating beef and fish and trying to keep a straight face whenever castle guests share their theories about the Loch Ness Monster.

But even as I dare to consider such a thing, the rest of me is screaming *no! It's a trap! Run!*

I can't say how long we stay like that, leaning against the porch railing in silence, when my father steps outside and invites us to come in and bunk down for the night in the big open loft of the cabin. We start to follow him back inside, but Ed hangs back, and I pause, too, and look up into his face in question.

"I want to thank ye, Wren, for yer courage—that ye didna hide yerself from me. 'Tis a gift, knowin' ye."

His voice is soft.

I should probably say something, but my heart is beating in such a panic, I couldn't find the words even if I knew what message I wanted to convey. I feel so confused.

All I can do is nod and dumbly follow my dad back inside. What could I admit to Ed? I'm glad, too, that I followed my instinct and let on who I really am, though to be honest that had as much to do with Ed's courage as mine. He befriended me first. He hinted at the ways he was different. I wouldn't have been brave enough, otherwise.

But I don't know how to say anything of this to him, and it's crowded inside the cabin. I take my turn brushing my teeth while my sister explains the plan for that evening.

Once we've all slept most of the day away, we're going to split into groups and investigate. Some of us will go down to the lake with Ed's camera equipment, while others will hike the lake area looking for signs of Eudora's operation. We're going to see what we can find.

And based on what we find…we're going to come up with a plan.

*

174

I awaken to the scent of roasted meat and join the others just as everyone's assembling and discussing who will be doing what. It's only mid-afternoon, but we need to get going if we're to have enough light to see by, even if that increases the possibility that we, too, could be seen.

We're breaking into three groups. One group will go out on the lake on Xalil's rowboat and use Ed's camera equipment to peer under the water. The other two groups, one led by Xalil, one by Jala, will scout around the lake looking for anything we can find that might be related to the water yagi operation.

Xalil and Jala have already observed Eudora coming and going near the north end of the lake, but they were never able to get close enough to see what she was doing, partly because they didn't want her to know they were spying on her, and partly because she kept disappearing.

Yes, *disappearing*.

No matter how close they crept, or how vigilantly they tracked her, somewhere near the north end of the lake she stepped out of their sight, only to emerge hours later and go back to her fortress. Subsequent searches of the area where she disappeared revealed nothing. We're hoping, with more of us searching, and with our extra-sharp dragon eyesight, that we'll spot something Xalil and Jala missed.

And since they haven't checked the area in a few weeks— not since they first spotted the dragon with the drag net, and turned their focus to recording footage of the flying creature's activities—there's a chance something has changed. Maybe Eudora has since left behind some trace of where's she's disappeared to, that Xalil and Jala wouldn't have been able to find weeks ago.

My sister quickly volunteers to go with Jala's group. My dad is interested to go out on the lake with Ed.

I've already gotten far closer than I ever wanted to the water yagi, so I don't want to go out on the boat. And I'm not particularly keen on ending up in the same group with my mother, who seems to still be upset with me. Since there are nine of us (my six family members, plus Ed, Jala, and Xalil) that means three persons per team. I volunteer to go with Jala and Zilpha, making a full team of three.

Ram decides to go with my dad and Ed, leaving my mother and Felix to scout around the lake with Xalil.

That much decided, we finish our dinner and suit up to head out, strapping on swords and daggers, and stowing flashlights and other gear in our backpacks. We're on Eudora's turf now, so we need to be prepared to encounter yagi.

Since we don't want to be seen in dragon form, not this close to Eudora's fortress, we don't dare fly, but there aren't any roads leading from the spy cabin to the lake. The ground is uneven due to the mountainous terrain, with treacherous crags and steep ravines, so we all stick together on the hike to the lake, following the guidance of Xalil and Jala, who've been wise enough to establish alternate safe routes so they don't wear a visible trail that might lead Eudora back to them.

I'm glad we decided to leave while we still have several hours of daylight. I can't imagine making the trek or attempting to find anything at the lake in the darkness.

Once we reach the shore, Xalil shows my dad the place where he hides his rowboat. Our group splits off from the others, heading around the lake in one direction, while Xalil takes Felix and my mother around the other way.

In spite of the danger, it's a lovely walk. The lake is deceptively peaceful, though the breeze across the lake's surface creates distorted, unnatural wave patterns—a sign that whatever is under the water is more powerful than what's above it. The occasional breaching water yagi serves as a grotesque reminder that we're not safe. This is not an innocent hike. Creatures swarm nearby, bred to kill us, and they outnumber us by a huge margin.

Jala and Zilpha and I stay alert for any sign of anything out of place in the woods—footprints, or anything that didn't come from nature. My sister and I, like all dragons, have exceptional eyesight, so even though Jala and her father have scouted around the lake for years, I still hope we might spot something their previous excursions have missed.

The lake is slightly oval in shape, a little over a mile wide east to west, a little less than a mile across north to south. My dad, brother, and Ed row out toward the middle of the lake. The wooden boat, though small and old, nonetheless seems sturdy enough. It bothers me, though, that they're out there in the midst of all those water yagi—creatures who exist for the purpose of killing them. I pause a few times on our hike to watch the men, and I hold my breath, hoping the yagi don't realize what's on the other side of the wooden hull floating above them.

While we don't know a great deal about yagi—their bodies evaporate quickly once you kill them, so we've never been able to study a dead one—we can tell certain things about them based on their behavior. They don't attack humans, only dragons, whether in human form or dragon form. How they know the difference is anybody's guess, but the most reasonable explanation seems to be that they identify us by smell.

Water yagi are a completely different species, though. Can they smell us underwater? I guess. Sharks can smell underwater—they can detect something like a single drop of blood in enough water to fill a backyard swimming pool. Can't they? Or is that just urban legend?

I'm pondering all these things as we're hiking through the woods, mostly quiet so we can focus on looking for things, and so we don't draw attention to ourselves. Granted, the men are in the boat in the middle of the lake where anyone might see them, so we're far from invisible, but from the shore they just look like a few guys out fishing.

You know, in the middle of remote Siberia.

Most importantly, do they *smell* like guys out fishing? Do the water yagi know the difference? Can water yagi smell things that aren't in the water? And what's going to happen when Ed lowers his camera into the water?

I reach an outcropping of jagged boulders overlooking the lake, where there aren't any trees or branches to obstruct my view, and I stop to watch the men. They've got the camera equipment out and they're preparing to lower it over the edge. Domed shapes writhe beneath the water's surface. Is it my imagination, or are the yagi more active and more thickly gathered in the part of the lake surrounding the boat?

What would happen if the yagi tipped the boat over in the middle of the lake? My dad and brother might be able to change into dragons and fly away, but what would become of Ed in the midst of so many water yagi?

Chapter Twenty-One

As I watch, Ed lowers the camera by the sturdy cable that connects it to the equipment on the boat. Its waterproof surface touches the water, sending concentric circles rippling out for only a short distance before the swarms of water yagi disrupt them.

I hold my breath, waiting for some response from the yagi. Their forms churn just below the surface of the water, but they make no move to attack.

My dad's got the screen balanced on his knees, but I can't see what he's looking at, not from this distance. Ram feeds more cable to Ed, who lowers the camera steadily, slowly.

"We should keep moving," Jala whispers to me. "The place where Eudora disappeared is still up ahead. We should try to reach it before it gets dark out. We'll stay close enough to the lake you can see if anything happens on the boat."

I nod and follow Jala and my sister, surprised by how reluctant I am to turn away from the men on the boat. I have a job to do—to search the shore for any sign of what Eudora's been up to. I need to focus on my assignment every bit as much as Ed is focused on his. With this reminder, I make it a point to scour the woods for some sign that Eudora, water yagi, or the mysterious other dragon has passed this way.

Nothing.

Through another break in the trees I see that my brother and Ed are rowing again. Ed's got the camera cable in one hand while my dad studies the picture on the monitor. Either he's guiding them northward across the lake based on whatever he sees on the screen, or he's trying to get them away from the clustering water yagi, which are swarming so thickly around to the boat the water seems to rise up around them in a sudden heap, and grasping hands tug at the oars as the rowboat nudges forward through their midst, lurching unevenly over the writhing bodies.

I wish I could see the screen. I wish I knew what was happening. The water yagi are certainly aware there's something above them, and they don't seem happy about it. But do they know the boat holds dragons? Or are they only irritated by the disruption? We don't know nearly enough about our enemy to fight them capably.

That's the catch. Even though Ed, my father, and my brother are trying to learn more about the water yagi on this expedition, doing so exposes them to unknown dangers. The rowboat bumps along, jostled by the swarming forms below the surface, and I wince with its every unnatural movement, bracing myself for the moment when the yagi decide to capsize the craft and swallow its sailors like the mythical sea monsters of old.

"Worried about Ed?" Zilpha asks, coming to a stop beside me.

"Yes. The water yagi are trying to tip the boat—look at the way they jostle it. Dad and Ram can fly away, but Ed can't."

"Ed's a big boy. He'll be fine."

"I know. He's strong. He's a strong swimmer. I just—" my hands clench into feeble fists as the boat lurches from side to side, the men adjusting their stances to steady it.

"You care about him," Zilpha says, as though she's finishing my sentence.

I open my mouth to protest, but when I look at her, Zilpha's smiling with that I-caught-you look that sisters are born to give sisters. Instead of getting into an argument we don't have time for anyway, I turn back in the direction we were headed. "Let's keep moving."

I try not to watch the men too closely, then—try not to give Zilpha any more reason to believe I care about Ed. Because if Zilpha thinks *I* care about Ed, she'll think she doesn't need to fall in love with him, and that's the opposite of what I want.

So I'm focusing on the ground, the trees, the rocks that jut up everywhere, jagged bits of mountain that don't lie down in smooth piles, probably because this area gets far more snow than rain, so the rocks have never been worn smooth by water and time, but lie frozen in the forms they took as they cracked from the heaving earth. They cast odd shadows, which lengthen as the sun sinks toward the western ridge.

I can understand how Eudora could so easily disappear in these woods. The rocks and trees are like statues. Eudora would need only stand still or duck behind one to blend in completely. I half expect her or yagi to step out from the shadows at any moment.

The thought runs uneasily up and down my spine, twitching to my fingertips, which ache to change into dragon talons—as fearsome as any enemy, and therefore safer.

But I don't want to be seen as a dragon, not if I can help it, not this close to Eudora's fortress. I try to tell myself we're fine, that everything will be okay, but I feel my concern rise like grave foreboding.

We're in unfamiliar territory, on our enemy's turf.

We're vastly outnumbered by yagi and water yagi.

And who knows how many dragons Eudora's recruited to her side?

I glance again toward the lake, hoping to see the reassuring sight of Ed and my dad and brother gathering helpful information, but instead I can see my dad and brother struggling to keep the boat from tipping, their legs braced against the sides as Ed leans over the front, hauling up the camera equipment quickly.

But not quickly enough.

The wooden hull rises upward, dripping, from the water. It tips unsteadily, and Ed leans back to help my father and brother balance it. But how do you balance a boat that's no longer *in* the water? It's like they're crowd surfing on the hands of the yagi. Ed and Ram take up oars, but the yagi are holding the vessel too high to row through the lake.

181

Instead, Ed and Ram swat at yagi hands with their wooden oars, beating the creatures on both side of the boat. It sinks back toward the water, slightly, then heaves again on only one side.

It's going over!

My dad and brother change into dragons—something I know they were holding off on doing unless they had no choice. But right now, any risk of being seen in dragon form takes a back seat to survival.

Ed drops his oar as he struggles to hold tight to the camera equipment. He leans away from the direction of the tipping boat even as my father and brother take hold of the small wooden craft in their taloned claws, and lift the boat, Ed and all, into the air.

They beat their wings, flying low across the lake. Having carried Ed myself, I know he's heavy even without a boat, but there are two of them doing the work, and it's not that far to shore. I watch, not wanting to blink, until they reach the southern shore and set down again.

"Look at your hands," Zilpha whispers in my ear.

I look, reflexively, before I even have a chance to think how odd her words are under the circumstances. And so I see, before they change back over to human, that my talons have grown long; my hands, red and scaly.

Self-conscious, I put my hands behind my back. They're back to human now, but I can feel my face has gone red. Not dragon red, just embarrassed. More than that…guilty.

"Were you going to fly to the rescue?" Zilpha asks.

"If necessary." I try to make my voice sound casual, and fail miserably, even though, honestly, what's wrong with my concern? Wouldn't anyone with half a heart care what happened out there on the lake?

Zilpha gives me a questioning look that says she doesn't understand, either. "Why don't you want to admit it?"

"Admit what?"

"That you're in love with Ed."

I open my mouth to protest, but only strangled sounds come out.

Zilpha continues. "It's not like we can't tell, Wren. We'd love to be happy for you, but not if you're not happy for yourself first."

The strangled sounds gasp toward something coherent. "We?" That one word is all I can manage. I'm still half terrified on Ed's behalf with the near-capsizing of the boat, and the men barely escaping, and part of me wonders what kind of footage they got on the camera, and I'm still pretty mostly sure I'm not in love with Ed, certainly not so much that anyone would notice.

But if Zilpha has noticed, and whoever else "we" might be, maybe Ed has noticed, too, which is not something I want, because it isn't going to make it any easier for me to say goodbye to him without hurting him.

Or me.

Fortunately Zilpha explains before my thoughts run away any further with my fears. "Mom and I have noticed and talked about it. I doubt the guys realize anything." Zilpha glances toward Jala, who's keeping a polite distance and investigating the same rocks and trees over and over while we talk. Bless her.

Zilpha continues with a quizzical look. "Does this have anything to do with you not wanting to turn into mom?"

I tip my head back and groan at the sky. "No. It's nothing against mom. I like mom just fine." I look back at Zilpha and meet her eyes, hoping to see understanding or at least sympathy, but instead it's just confusion. "I don't want to marry. I've never wanted to marry."

"Why not? It's our duty."

"It's your duty—yours and Rilla's. There were never going to be enough dragon men to go around anyway. I opted out from the beginning so you and Rilla could both have dibs. You'd think you'd be grateful."

Zilpha still looks confused.

183

I grasp her by the shoulders and try to drill the information through her eyes with a stern look. "You have always been the one who was going to marry, just like Rilla is the one who's going to get her college degree, whatever it takes, nothing will stand in her way. That's who you are, and who Rilla is. I'm the one who is *not* those things."

We stand there for who knows how long, and honestly, I don't get why this is so difficult for my sister to grasp. She's my sister, my litter mate, my sort-of-triplet hatchling buddy. This is how it's always been, each of us differentiating ourselves off against the other. When you're triplets, it's a matter of survival, of becoming someone who's not just one-third of three. We made ourselves known by our preferences, our favorite colors, individual styles, preferred foods, whatever.

We each have our labels that define who were are. We're three different colors when we're in dragon form—I'm red, Rilla's robin's egg blue, Zilpha's a sort of magenta red-violet. Rilla was the studious one, Zilpha the sociable one, and I'm the one who would not be defined by either of those labels.

But instead of experiencing a moment of enlightenment, Zilpha blinks at me. "Are you mad?"

"No." Confused, maybe, but not mad.

"Are you mad at Mom?"

"No."

"You should tell her that."

"Fine," I shrug. Mom's not around right now, so there's no way for me to have that conversation. "We should go back to the cabin and see what the guys found."

"No," Zilpha argues, "we should continue our search. The menfolk are doing their part. We need to do ours."

Jala sidles closer now that I've released my sister's shoulders. "We're almost to the place where Eudora disappeared. There's still some light out. Let's get moving."

"I guess that's the best choice," I relent, even though I'm pretty sure the men went back to the cabin, so I want to go back to make sure Ed is okay, and to learn what they found. But saying so would only reinforce my sister's zany theory that I'm in love with Ed. And we *do* need to find out what Eudora's been up to.

We continue on. The sun has dipped somewhere beyond the craggy crest of the surrounding mountains, but the sky still holds a gray-lit, otherworldly glow. I've noticed this the further north we go, and the closer the days march toward the summer equinox. We're far north. Crazy far north, at a more northerly latitude than even the Scottish Highlands. It doesn't get properly dark here this time of year until much later, and it doesn't stay dark for very long.

Instead there's this long spell of twilight, belonging neither to the day nor the night, kind of like the way water yagi are neither human nor cockroach nor fish.

Okay, now I'm creeping myself out.

So we're hiking through the spooky half-darkness forever, and the closer we get to where Eudora disappeared, the slower we go, on account of we have to search more carefully and don't want to miss anything. And we've got our flashlights out now, the lights bobbing around through the woods like the bowed heads of alien beings, beams trained on the forest floor, dipping and ducking behind every rock and tree.

Jala's ventured farther north, deeper into the woods in the direction of Eudora's fortress, although that's still something like three miles away, and Zilpha's crept nearer to the lake shore, where I don't want to go but at the same time I can't turn my back on my sister for fear the water yagi will reach up and grab her off the bank.

So while I'm searching the vast zone in between them, trying not to be afraid of the deepening darkness, and thinking before long we ought to catch up to Felix and Xalil and my mother, I hear a noise in the bushes from over where Jala was searching.

I look that way just in time to hear her shrill scream, but I can't see Jala anywhere, and the light from her flashlight is gone.

Chapter Twenty-Two

"Jala!" Zilpha and I shout in unison, both of us bounding through the woods in the direction of her scream.

I reach the area first, but I don't see anything. I'm casting about with my flashlight when I see three more beams moving swiftly through the woods toward us.

"Wren? Zilpha? Are you okay?" It's my mother's voice. They've circled around the other side of the lake.

Xalil's voice is mixed with hers. "Jala? Girls?"

"We're over here," I call out, even as their questions grow in volume—they seem more concerned about our safety and whether anyone's injured, than the risk of giving away our presence to Eudora or any of her spies who might be about. And their flashlight beams grow brighter as they near us, even as I search the woods, looking for Jala.

"Oh, ow. Yes, I think I'm okay." Jala's voice echoes distantly from somewhere, but I can't see where. It almost sounds like she's...below us?

I turn my flashlight beam in the direction where her words seemed to originate. There's no one there, but I'm close enough now I can see that what looked, from a distance, like the skeletal outline of the limbs of a fallen tree, is, in fact, the skeletal outline of...a skeleton.

Several skeletons, actually.

Not human. Bigger than human. Mostly elk, I think, and maybe bear.

Felix runs toward the bones, which are lit by the beam of my flashlight and now his, as well.

"Careful!" Jala calls up from somewhere still out of sight. "Watch your step or you'll land on me!"

"Where are you?" Felix asks.

"Turn your lights off."

We obey Jala's request, even though it seems strange. Only in the absence of our light beams can we see the faint glow of Jala's light shining upward from somewhere underground.

Felix and I approach the spot cautiously.

"Are you sure you're okay?" Felix asks.

"I scraped my arm on the rock as I fell," Jala confesses. "And I thought I might have twisted my ankle, but maybe I just wrenched it. I can put weight on it. Can you see to help me up?"

"I'd rather help myself down." Felix sits on a lip of stone, then disappears downward.

I train my light on the spot.

There's an opening in the ground, a natural fissure in the stone, like a narrow, deep ravine, no more than four or five feet long, and hardly two feet wide at its widest point. But it's deep—maybe ten feet deep, and the floor slopes off out of sight under the lip of stone I'm standing on.

"Jala? Are you okay?" Xalil finally reaches the rest of us. My mother and Zilpha have come up and had a peek, then ducked back to investigate the animal skeletons while Jala assures her grandfather she isn't seriously hurt.

Felix offers to boost her back up, and she stands on his bent knees and reaches for my hands. I pull her up, then hop down in her place as Felix shines his flashlight beam around the subterranean space.

"It's a cave," he observes. "A deep cave."

"Any sign of Eudora down there?" Mom asks from above.

"Nothing that I can see." Felix has his light trained on one rock wall, which is jutted and uneven. Footprints mar the dirt. I start to head that direction to investigate when my mom's words pull me up short.

"I think you need to come back up from down there," my mom informs us. She's looking down into the hole from above, her flashlight beam joining ours.

"But look, Mom. Footprints," Felix points out.

"Yes—and you're leaving footprints of your own. Did you think of that? Come up out of there. It's getting late—that dragon could come back anytime, and if you're in his cave he might leave and never come back, and we'll never know who he was or if there were any more of him."

Felix helps boost me up toward my mother, but asks, "Do you really think this is the dragon's cave? The entrance isn't big enough for a dragon, not in dragon form."

"The dragon must come and go as a human. Look at these elk bones. They're recent kills, the marrow sucked out, but the bones aren't fully dried." My mom catches Felix by the hand as he leaps toward the lip of the cave, bounding atop a small boulder from below. She pulls him out.

My brother and I inspect the bones, which look similar to those we've left behind after dinner the last few nights. "Sure looks like a dragon's been here," I agree. Either that or some other large, carnivorous beast.

"This is the same area where Eudora disappeared before," Xalil informs us solemnly. "She must have gone into that cave, perhaps to meet with the dragon. It's getting late—near the time the dragon arrived before. We should hide and watch from a distance."

Everyone agrees Xalil's idea is a good one, but my mother also suggests some of us could go back to the cabin to find out what the men have learned about the lake.

I volunteer to be part of the group that returns. Don't get me wrong—I'm as curious as anyone about what's been going on at this cave, and with the dragon, and everything, but far more than that, I want to make sure Ed's okay and find out what he learned.

Besides which, I know Zilpha and Felix are both hoping this new dragon might be a potential mate, so they want to stick around to make sure the dragon doesn't get away, and maybe get a head start on flirting with him or her.

And much as I want Zilpha to get together with Ed, mostly I just want Zilpha to be happy.

Jala wants to rest her ankle a bit longer, so she agrees to stay behind with Felix and Zilpha while Xalil leads me and my mother back toward the cabin. Xalil scouts ahead, finding the path in the darkness, and my mother and I follow at a bit of a distance, keeping his flashlight beam in sight.

We walk in silence for a bit. Once we're well out of earshot of those we've left behind, I inform my mother bluntly, "I'm not mad at you." And then, when she doesn't respond right away, I ask, "Are you mad at me?"

"I'm not mad. I'm…concerned."

"Concerned why? How? For my safety?"

"I'm always concerned for my kids' safety," my mom admits, "now more than ever, since we're on this dangerous mission. But no, I'm concerned you may be making a choice you'll later regret."

Her words hit me kind of low, like a punch to the stomach, and for a few minutes I'm quiet again, trying to digest what she's said. It's funny, because this whole time, pretty much from the moment we got to Nattertinny Castle, I've felt like I need to be on my guard, to protect myself from falling into something I'd regret. Or starting something.

But perhaps I have started something, the very thing I've been trying not to start.

So finally, sick of stewing over what she must mean, I ask, "What choice?"

Mom sighs. "Ed."

"Ed." I repeat. Zilpha had said she and my mom both agreed. "You and Zilpha think that I…" I swallow back the rest of the words. I can't say them. I've fought against them for too long to say them now.

"Why are you so scared of it?" My mother asks in a whisper, as though she's afraid she'll frighten me away from the subject if she speaks at full volume.

She doesn't say what "it" is, but I know. Marriage. And I've thought about this a lot lately, mostly because my mother and now my sister keep bringing the subject up. So I put it in the best words I can. "Remember how you used to tell us stories about your childhood and going away to Saint Evangeline's School for Girls, and how one of the worst part wasn't the food or the dreary cold or even being away from your family—"

"Those were all the worst parts," my mom assures me.

"But the *worst* worst part was that they made you wear shoes."

"Ugh, yes. That was the worst. Not in a big way, but in a constantly oppressive sort of way."

"That's what it feels like, Mom. That's what I'm afraid of."

"Shoes?"

"No. Being…fettered. Shackled. Constrained. Restricted. I mean, I haven't even ever been on my own yet. I've never yet been *me*. I can't be a *we* until I've learned who *I* am. I'm not ready to be fettered."

"Love doesn't fetter you."

"Not love, Mom. *Marriage*."

"Marriage?" My mom suddenly sounds horrified. "Marriage? First of all, no, marriage doesn't shackle you. But Wren, Sweet Baby Doll," (Don't ask me why my mom sometimes calls us kids *Sweet Baby Doll*. For being a wicked cool dragon, she can sometimes be embarrassingly sentimental.) "You don't have to marry Ed. Not anytime soon." She laughs. "You're both immortal. He's lived hundreds of years, I think he'd be willing to wait a few more. Just don't push him away, or hurt him. Don't shut down a good thing."

So then we tromp through the woods in silence a lot longer, because I don't know how to respond to what my mom is saying. Aren't love and marriage the same thing? Love, marriage…a baby in a baby carriage? I'm pretty sure that's what I've always heard.

And anyway, hasn't that been the whole point of finding dragon men all along, so we can marry them and have dragon babies? And isn't that part of what I'm afraid of—liking a guy, a real dragon guy, and then—boom—babies.

Before I've nearly got the issue sorted, we arrive back at the spy cabin (I know it doesn't feel as though it took nearly as long on the way back as it did on the way out, but we aren't looking for signs of where Eudora may have disappeared anymore, and we walked in silence a good bit).

The men have the camera footage playing on the large monitor as Xalil and my mom and I enter the room behind them. The screen is filled with the swarming shapes of the yagi. They are even creepier up close.

Though I'm repelled by the sight, I hurry over for a closer look.

"I don't see any fish in the lake," Ram observes aloud. "I think they must have eaten them all, and now they've gone cannibalistic."

"What?" I hadn't thought about water yagi actually eating anything. Especially not each other. "I can't imagine that tasting good."

"You missed it," my dad explains. "The camera caught a yagi eating another yagi. Ram's theory makes sense—the lake is overpopulated with these creatures. They've eaten all the fish, so now they're desperate enough to turn on each other."

Ed's sitting in the chair in front of the computer, with the camera equipment connected by cables, zooming in here and there and fiddling with the brightness settings to try to improve the picture. I clamp my hands on his shoulders. "You can't go in that lake."

"But I have to. We were just discussin' the plan before ye arrived."

"Ed!" There might be a note of panic in my voice. Just a tiny one. "The water yagi will *eat* you."

"Not if I'm a sea dragon. They canna pierce me armor."

"You don't know for sure they can't. Maybe those other water yagi were early models, and these new improved ones can eat you just like they eat each other." As I'm talking, a water yagi swims close to the camera, teeth bared, as if to reinforce the threat.

"But I have to go in the water," Ed explains patiently, pointing to the screen as the underwater scene unfolds. "We found where they're comin' from. There's an underground stream that's spittin' out small ones. That's why the larger ones are feedin' here—these are the newest, weakest yagi. All I have to do is swim up that stream, and I'll find the source of the water yagi. Then I can destroy it."

"And we've got to act quickly," my dad adds, so close on the tails of Ed's words that I don't even have time to voice the fear that's freezing inside my veins at the thought of what might happen to Ed in the lake. "Now that Ram and I have changed into dragons, we may have been seen. Eudora may even now be making preparations to launch an attack against us, or to move her operation. If she does that, we'll lose our chance to destroy it."

"I'm ready." Ed stands and turns toward the door.

"Wait. What? Just like that?" I head after him.

He turns part way around, but he's still headed outside. "I've got me sword, got me daggers. Might as well go now. There's no gain in waitin', and plenty to lose."

Ed's plan seems crazy dangerous to me, but my dad and Ram act like it's the only sensible option.

"I want to bring the camera equipment again," Ram notes, disconnecting it from the computer. "That way we can see how you're doing underwater."

"Won't be able to see me fer long." Ed notes, but doesn't argue further.

While my dad helps my brother with the camera equipment, I tug Ed by the sleeve out to the porch. If he's going in that dangerous water, I need to say what I can quickly. Who knows if I'll get another chance?

Ed looks at me with that familiar raised eyebrow of curiosity, the one that says he knows I have something to say, and he wants to hear it.

"I'm afraid." I announce without preamble.

Ed raises the other eyebrow as if to open the floodgates of confession.

But I'm stuck. I'm not sure what I'm confessing, exactly—just that I might sort of somewhat care about Ed, and love and marriage may not be the same thing, but what do I know about either?

"Yer afeared? Of the lake?"

"Well, that too," I acknowledge. I'm afraid the lake might claim Ed before I get a chance to explain myself—that he might never know how I truly feel. But all that's stopped up by the fact that *I* don't know how I truly feel.

Ed takes my hands and looks at me with concern. When I swallow several times repeatedly and still can't make words come out, he makes his best attempt to fill in the gaps with what he knows from what I've said before. "Yer afeared of gettin' pulled under by something below ye."

I stare at him for one dumb moment as I realize it's the same thing, isn't it? I'm afraid of being fettered, of being chained down, pulled under, of never rising up and becoming who I could be. I'm afraid of marriage pulling me down, holding me back. I'm afraid of loving Ed, because it would be like swimming in a lake that might hold water yagi. It would make me vulnerable to the thing I fear most—of drowning even though I can fly.

The confession comes out in broken, stuttering gasps, while rogue tears sneak down my cheeks, betraying the depth of my feelings. "Yes. I care about you, Ed. You're very special to me, but I just can't—" I shake my head, searching for the words that will help him understand. "I want to fly."

"Aye." His voice is rough and rumbly, but soft. "I want ye to fly, Wren. That's who ye are."

There's a sound at the door, and I glance behind me to see my dad and brother with the camera equipment, on their way out the door. They're coming outside. We've got things to do—water yagi to defeat, all the water of the world to save from them forever.

Ed gives my hand a final squeeze. "I understan'. I wouldna presume to hold ye back. Fly free, Wren. I havena got wings."

The last bit of his words are buried as my parents and brother emerge from the house in a bustle of preparations and chatter. I catch the last of Ed's statement with half an ear as I turn my face away from my family and hastily wipe away all trace of my tears before I face them. But even as I do so, I realize what Ed said.

He hasn't got wings.

Chapter Twenty Three

Wings.

That wasn't what I was referring to, not intentionally, not at all. But it fits, doesn't it? Or does it? Ed's already down the front cabin steps, hiking along the trail beside my father and brother, carrying the row boat between them, his strong shoulders taut as he totes the heavy vessel as if it weighs nothing.

He is so strong, and so determined to defeat the enemy that haunts me, no matter the risk.

I fall into step beside my mom, who gives me a look that says she can see my tears, never mind that I wiped them away.

"Everything okay? Did you talk to Ed?"

"I talked to Ed," I confirm, watching Ed carry the boat ahead of us. The sinking feeling inside me says that whatever he took away from our conversation, wasn't the same thing I intended. "I'm not sure if everything's okay."

"Care to tell me about it?"

"Not yet. I need to think." I study Ed, walking in front of us, has calf muscles taut and well-defined, everything about him nearly perfect, as I try to analyze what he said. My heart is beating with this crazy sense of panic like I should be alarmed by his words, and I have to tell myself to calm down.

But maybe I shouldn't calm down.

Maybe I should panic.

Because if I understood Ed correctly, he thinks I said the reason I don't want to marry him is because I don't want to be weighed down by a guy who can't fly. Like maybe without him, I can go places I couldn't go with him.

And while I didn't mean that—didn't even consider he might interpret my words that way—in some ways, isn't it all still the same thing? I don't want to marry because I don't want to be weighed down, chained down, fettered. Regardless of whether it's because of Ed's winglessness, or just his presence, it's the same thing, isn't it?

So then I ask my mom that question that I've been wrestling with for days now. "Mom, are dragons relics? Do we even belong in this world?"

My mom doesn't look shocked, but smiles almost as though she understands why I'd ask. "Yes, we belong."

"How do you know?"

"Because for a long time, I didn't think we belonged at all. I didn't think I should marry your father and create a new generation of dragons—I thought dragons were evil."

"Evil?"

"That's how we're portrayed in so many stories."

We're stomping along in the mostly-darkness behind the men. I can just see Ed's strong back ahead of us, mostly out of earshot. "But that's only because greedy people made up those stories. They're lies. Lies to make people hate us and destroy us so we can't protect our people," I clarify.

"Precisely. We are remnants from an enchanted age, echoes of a world that once was and could be again, if the world would stop hunting us. We're not pests. We were the true stewards of the earth from before the age of humans. And, I might argue, we kept it far better than they do."

"So…we're not relics?" I know that's what she's trying to say, but she almost makes it sound like we're even more antiquated than I'd assumed.

"We come from a *greater* age, Wren. We come from the age of dragons."

My mother's voice is infused with a sort of wistful pride I've not often heard from her. "But the real reason we belong, the reason why we have a place in this world, even if we're a little ancient and outdated, is because we need each other, and our people need us. You know, your grandmother Faye didn't want to be a dragon anymore, either. She went to Eudora to become truly human, but then she realized Eudora was wrong. And then my father rescued her, and she laid my egg, and she had someone to care about, more than just herself and the abstract concept of belonging. She had a child—me—and it gave her life purpose."

"So, if I lay an egg, my life will have purpose?"

"No. Well, yes, but you don't have to lay an egg to have a purpose, though the seeds of the future lie dormant inside you until you give them life. You just have to learn to love— yourself, another person, another dragon."

The last couple of my mom's words get completely lost as we look over our heads at a streak of fiery light. A blaze of yellow and gold, orange-tipped like a flame, shoots across the sky, headed toward the northern end of the lake.

The dragon.

Ahead of us, Ram looks like he's about to change into a dragon and take off after it. My mom runs up and catches him even as my dad holds him by the arm, tethering him to the earth.

"Don't go!" Mom tells Ram. "Felix and Zilpha are lying in wait at the cave. They're hiding. They'll watch the dragon and follow it. If you fly up there, you'll spook it."

My brother has this crazed look on his face like it's taking all his restraint not to change into a dragon. He's even sort of panting—which is really bizarre because Ram is always completely stoic. He doesn't get upset or emotional or caught up over anything.

But right now, he really, really wants to go after that dragon.

And I know why. He hopes it's a girl dragon. Or even if it's a boy dragon, he hopes maybe it could lead him to a potential wife.

In my head, theoretically, I've always known all my siblings wanted to find mates. But seeing it now, the strain on my brother's face, the way he watches the dragon fly past and then stares after it in the direction it disappeared, the visible battle on Ram's face as he fights the urge to fly after the creature—it gives me a new perspective. It's like the difference between hungry and *starving*. There's wanting-to-get-married and then there's *wanting-to-get-married*.

And I almost feel a little like I've been missing the point this whole time.

But we're almost to the lake already, and the guys have picked up their pace as the trees open up toward the lake and the walking is easier. Also I suspect Ram is hurrying because he hopes if he gets to the lake in time, he might catch another glimpse of the yellow dragon.

After a bit more walking the men reach the shore and lower the boat into the water, hopping in from atop the highest rocks, just out of the reach of the grasping hands of the water yagi.

It's completely dark out now, as dark as it can get in the middle of the Siberian night.

"Let's walk around toward the north shore," my mother suggests. "But we'll have to be careful not to spook the fiery dragon."

The men are preparing the camera and grasping the oars, soon to push off, and I feel this frantic sense that I'm not ready for them to leave yet. I'm not ready for Ed to go in the water, to face the teeming yagi, not yet.

"Are you sure that's wise? Maybe we should just go in the boat, too." I suggest, in a voice loud enough for the men to hear.

Ed looks back at me with surprise. "The lake's full of yagi." He knows I'm afraid of them, and it's clear in his voice he can't fathom why I'd want any closer to them.

"I know." What I don't say—what I can't bring myself to say, is that Ed's on the boat, so that's where I want to be, never mind that the lake is teeming with creatures bred to kill me.

For a long moment, Ed and I look at each other in silence. I'm wrestling with all the unspoken things I don't know how to say, and he's giving me that patient look that says he's waited six hundred years to hear me speak, and he'll wait as long as it takes.

Yes, he has a real look for that.

We're in the midst of this silent communication when a streak like a shooting star lights the woods on the far side of the lake, and the yellow dragon rises up above the trees, flying swiftly south, nearly over our heads and on into the distance.

My brother Ram kicks his shoes off.

"What are you doing?" my dad asks.

"I've got to go after it."

"But Felix is after it," my mother notes. Sure enough, I see my little brother's scarlet-red form rise up from the north shore, into the air, and past us as he flies after the dragon.

"I've got to go," Ram says again. "I wasn't going to be much help with this project. You'll be fine." He looks after the red light that is Felix, already growing small in the distance. "I've got to go."

He leaps into the air, morphing into the form of an indigo-blue dragon, and flying after the other two.

"Well." My father's lips form a thin line. "Eudora's not likely to miss that show. Let's get moving."

"Maybe I should come in the boat," I volunteer. "Now that Ram's gone?"

My mother's hiding a hint of smile. "I think that's a fine idea. I'm still going to tromp around to the northern shore and see if I can't find out what's become of Zilpha and Jala."

I think she thinks I just want to be in the boat because of Ed, so of course she's encouraging that. Maybe there's something to her theory, but that's the least of my concerns right now. I've *got* to get in the boat. And quickly. We need to destroy the water yagi before Eudora shows up to investigate how her fiery dragon got chased away.

Clambering out onto one of the high rocks, I reach for Ed. He takes secure hold of my wrists and I clasp his as well. Rather than think about the yagi swarming beneath my feet, I gaze into Ed's eyes—into the steady, timeless eyes of a dragon, the first dragon I've ever known outside of my own family. Something inside my heart swells with the joy of knowing and being known.

I step into the boat. Ed holds me with one arm, steady against his solid body, while he uses his other hand to lever the oar, helping my father push the boat away from the rocks.

"Settle in, now. It's no time fer an accident," Ed warns me once we're safely away from the rocks. He keeps hold of my arm until I'm safely seated. Then he and my dad row out to the northern end of the lake, their oars heaving through the churning water, moving the boat forward at a rapid clip.

Their rhythm slows as we reach the northern end of the lake. I've been fiddling with the camera equipment, doing what I can to ready it to watch Ed's progress. I'm really not comfortable with what he's about to do. I mean, I know we need to destroy the operation that makes the water yagi. And we need to do it soon. And Ed's really the best man for the job, maybe the only man.

It's just that he's doing it *for me*. He wouldn't even have known about the water yagi if I hadn't told him. He only ever investigated them in the first place because he knew they scared me. Then there's that whole part where he could die an ugly, nasty death, being eaten alive by these unnatural creatures.

So I guess it only makes sense I'm not comfortable with what's about to happen.

Ed, however, doesn't falter. He shucks off his shoes and in a moment is stripped to his kilt, ready to go.

He is so gorgeous.

While Ed prepares to get in the water, my dad starts lowering the camera equipment into place. I'm holding the small monitor, and now it lights up with a view of the creatures beneath us. I can see the outline of the cave or underwater stream or whatever it is that Ed thinks the creatures are coming from. It's a murky outline with only darkness beyond. And Ed's going to go there.

I don't like it.

"All ready then?" Ed asks, his body poised as though he's about to dive in.

"It's so dangerous," I admit, almost in spite of myself.

"It's got to be done," Ed reminds me patiently.

"But what if something happens to you?"

Ed shrugs. "I've lived a long life. Donna suppose the world would much miss me."

His words are so blunt, so unexpected, for a moment I'm too stunned to even know how to reply.

And then he dives into the water.

That's it. No good-bye, or reassurances, or anything. I mean, I guess my dad gave Ed a sharp nod, kind of like a signal that everything was ready. And, granted, we weren't getting anywhere with our conversation, not any further than we've ever gotten, but still.

He's gone and he might never come back, and I'm not okay with that.

Something desperate heaves inside of me.

Ed! Where is Ed? Is he okay?

I study the small screen in my hands, which is now my last link to Ed. My dad trained the camera toward the cave opening, and there he is. Ed is swimming. I can see clearly as he swims—in Loch Ness Monster form—swiftly toward the cave opening, then through, and out of sight.

"Now what?" I ask as my father, who watched Ed's progress on the screen from over my shoulder, sits down on the row boat bench seat beside me.

"Now we wait."

I'm not satisfied with his answer.

"Do you think he'll be okay?"

"He's got a better chance of succeeding than anyone else." My dad states succinctly. That's his way. He doesn't make false promises or offer hollow platitudes. And while his assessment is, I'm sure, correct, it still offers me little reassurance.

We sit there in silence for what feels like forever, and my concern grows. I need Ed to survive, to come back to me.

I need Ed.

But all I see on the screen are writhing water yagi. Nor is there any sign of activity elsewhere. At one point I think I catch a glimpse of my mom through the trees on the north shore of the lake, near the cave, but it's wicked dark out, so who knows?

On top of my fear that Ed might not come back, I'm trying not to let my fear of the water yagi get the best of me. That's not easy, considering that I'm in a boat, surrounded by water that's roiling with their bodies all around us, and the screen on my lap shows hideous underwater footage of their teeth, their grasping hands, and their unrelenting hunger.

I can't say how many yagi I've seen eat other yagi—more than I want to think about—when a wave surges beneath us with such suddenness, one moment we're sitting calmly in the boat, and the next we're gripping the seat with both hands as the fragile craft rises twenty feet in the air, shooting up on a wave that's almost like a geyser, or tsunami, or something very violent and aquatic.

I'm aware of several things all at once.

One, the lake water lit up, an eerie purplish-orange color that doesn't belong to nature any more than the water yagi.

And two, that wave wasn't caused by the yagi and their boat-tipping antics. It was caused by a power surge, an explosion, something so strong, it made my eardrums pop and shocked all the water yagi in the lake.

Their bodies clutter the lake's surface like so many dead fish. They're floating in thick layers, yagi upon yagi, all around us, unmoving. So gross.

I'm not sure if they're dead, or just stunned. At any moment they might come back to life, like zombie water yagi—in case water yagi weren't creepy enough.

But far more than zombie water yagi, I'm worried about Ed. The screen has gone black—no doubt the explosion ruined the camera equipment—and I have no idea where Ed is or even if he's hurt. I've lost my last link to him, the last tenuous thread that kept me from freaking out.

Here's what I know: that explosion was powerful—so powerful, all the yagi in the lake are floating lifelessly all around me. I don't think anything in the water survived. Our boat rose up on a wave and smacked back down, but more than that, a concussive force like wind blew up from the water and slapped me. And I'm not the one *in* the water.

"Ed?" I call out, looking all around for some sign of him, but there's nothing but these stunned yagi everywhere. "Ed?"

Seconds tick by—sickening seconds that I fear could mean the difference between life and death. Where is Ed? What if he's injured, hurting, trapped, alone? What if he needs me?

I stand on trembling feet and balance myself against my father's shoulder as I kick off my shoes.

"What are you doing?" my dad asks.

"I've got to find Ed."

My dad gives me this look like I've gone completely mad, but I don't have time to argue with him. I've waited too long already. How long has it been? Twenty seconds? Thirty? A minute?

Pinching my eyes shut against the sight of prone water yagi coating the surface of the lake, I rise up on dragon wings, point my noise toward the water, and dive.

Chapter Twenty-Four

Even stunned and lifeless, the water yagi are creepy, especially considering they're floating several layers thick. I dive past them, wincing, hoping they won't jostle back to life, roused by my brushing against them.

But honestly, the water yagi are the least of my concerns. Once I'm under the water, I open my eyes and look in the direction of the cave. It's completely dark, but I turn up the glow of my scales (fortunately a sense of urgency is an excellent catalyst for scale glow) and I can discern the cave opening deep in the water. The current feels like it's streaming from there, too, so I know it's the right spot.

I can't hold my breath anywhere near as long as Ed can, so I don't waste any time. I swim for the cave, into it, through it, through some kind of underground tunnel full of water which, to my disappointment, doesn't appear to have any pockets of air anywhere along its length.

Air is important.

My lungs are burning, pleading for air. It's all too reminiscent of the time when the water yagi attacked me on the Caspian Sea—the event that started this whole adventure.

I swim for all I'm worth, which isn't that impressive. Ed is so much better at swimming than I am. I just hope he's okay. I hope I can find him.

I hope I'm not too late.

I'm swimming, half blind from the darkness and lack of oxygen, swimming for all I'm worth, when finally, the darkness of the tunnel ahead of me gives way to a flicker of orange light. I swim toward it, faster now, desperately, because I know my lungs are going to burst or I'm going to pass out, or whatever it is that happens when a dragon runs out of oxygen underwater.

The orange glow grows bigger. It looks like fire. It's not just in front of me, but up, above me. I crane my neck and strain upward.

My face breaks the surface and I gasp for air. There are water yagi here, too, floating lifelessly on the water, but they're smaller and fewer in number. Juvenile yagi, probably from the source Ed was seeking to destroy.

There's also smoke—swirling white smoke, growing ever thicker, rising from the burning thing on the shore.

The smoke is mostly swirling high in the cave. I keep my face low, near the surface of the water, and suck in deep breaths as I scan the cave for some sign of Ed. I'm in a vast space. The ceiling is somewhere high above me, lost to the smoke. The stream opens up like an underground lake, with a beach in front of me. On one side of the beach is a massive tangle of tubes and wires and gears and parts and shiny metal. It's on fire—a slow, smoldering fire—but I suspect this massive contraption may have been the source of the explosion that stunned all the water yagi.

And I also suspect Ed was behind making the explosion happen. But where is he now?

My oxygen levels mostly restored, I swim swiftly toward the bank. I'm nearly ashore when I spot Ed, in human form, lying on his back, feet pointed toward the smoldering contraption as though he was thrown back when the explosion occurred.

Has he been lying here all this time?

Is he even breathing?

I run to him, turning into a human so I can assess his injuries, and cup his face in my hands. "Ed? Ed! Are you okay?"

Nothing. His skin is warm, but then again, the cave is hot from the burning contraption, which stinks like seared water yagi, which is even nastier than un-burnt water yagi. Ed doesn't move, doesn't groan or twitch or anything.

"Ed! Wake up! We've got to get out of here!" It's occurred to me that, besides the possibility that the water yagi might rouse to life at any moment and pull us underwater or eat us, there's a strong likelihood the burning contraption might not be done exploding. Even if it is, the fire is using up our oxygen, which can't be good. We're in a highly unstable place.

I really, really need Ed to wake up.

My tears splash against his face as I grope his neck with numb fingers, trying to find a pulse. He's got to live. He's *got* to. I haven't ever had a chance to tell him how I feel about him. It can't be too late.

What was it he said before he dived into the lake? Something about the world not even missing him? He knew he might not make it out alive, didn't he? But he did it for me.

He did it because he loves me.

And I never got a chance to tell him how I really feel.

He has to wake up!

Besides that, he has to get up so I can get him out of here. How are we supposed to escape, anyway? The only way out that I know of is the way I came in, and I barely made it through then, before I was tired and breathless. And I wasn't trying to haul Ed's lifeless body. I don't think I can make it with him, not if he's unconscious.

But there's no way I'm going to leave him.

Sometime in the midst of thinking all these things, my hand finds a place on his neck that's throbbing with a sort of steady throb my fingers recognize as a pulse. I cram my hand against it to make sure, then realize maybe I'm cutting off the blood flow to his brain, which probably isn't a very nice way to repay him, considering he destroyed the contraption that was spitting out yagi, and from the looks of it killed off all the yagi in the lake at the same moment.

"Ed!" Now that I know he's alive, I'm back to screaming at him. "Come on! You've got to wake up!" And it occurs to me that I should also check if he's breathing, so I watch his chest closely. It's an awesome chest, all muscular and manly. But it's not moving.

Now I feel like a total idiot. I have to give Ed rescue breaths! Of course! I should have thought of this long seconds ago.

I pull in a deep breath (I'm still catching my breath, myself, having just crawled out of the lake maybe ten or twenty seconds ago—yes, I know it feels like longer than that, but that's because everything is so intense right now) and I clamp my lips around Ed's lips, and blow.

Okay, so I had my eyes shut that time, so I don't know if it did anything. I take another deep breath and try again, this time with my eyes on his chest.

And…it sort of rises a little.

I check his pulse.

Still pulsing away. That's good, right? I tip his head back further in an attempt to open up his airway a bit more. Then I suck in my deepest breath yet, clamp my lips around his, and blow like crazy.

His chest rises, a good clear rise, this time, and then he makes a strangled gagging sound, followed by coughing.

I have never been so happy to have someone cough in my face.

"Ed? Are you alive?" When he doesn't answer, I clamp my lips around his again, because, frankly, I'm feeling a little panicked right now, and regretful that I didn't think of the rescue breathing sooner, and also because, gagging and coughing aside, I rather like having my lips on his.

And also because, long before the lip clamping has a chance to get awkward, Ed's conscious again underneath me. At least, I'm pretty sure he's conscious, because he's kissing me back.

Did I mention that I'm kissing him? I must have forgotten to note that. We'll blame the lack of oxygen, and also my total absorption in the task at hand, which is to kiss the very hot Scotsman who I moments ago thought I might never see again, and then moments after that feared was dead.

In between kisses, I ask him, "Are you okay?"

"Never better."

I giggle. Yes, this is what I've been reduced to. Me, mighty dragon, giggling and kissing. I knew love was going to turn me into mush. I knew it! I just don't mind so much right now, on account of the kissing.

"Wren! Ed? Are you down there?" Mom's voice echoes from somewhere not so far away.

"Mom?" Sadly, I have to break off kissing Ed long enough to stare into the smoke (wow, that smoke is getting thick up there) to find where my mom's voice is coming from.

"Wren? Honey—follow my voice. You've got to get out of there!"

I look down at Ed, panicked again now because while I was having a romantic interlude and otherwise not paying attention, the cave has been filling with thick smoke, and the water yagi contraption is sparking and sputtering and making ominous noises like another explosion might be imminent.

"We've got to get out of here," I inform Ed, just in case he didn't hear my mom. "Can you move?"

"I dunno." Ed clambers to his feet and I stand alongside him, but now we're in the thick smoke, so I bend low again as Ed takes my hand and we run together toward Mom's voice.

"Wren? Can you hear me? Are you coming? Are you okay?"

I try to answer her, but it's all I can do to cough. Then we're clambering up some rocks and Mom's still shouting for us (it's a good thing she's shouting, too, because I can't see anything but white smoke and Ed's shoulder two feet in front of me). We sort of stumble into Mom all of a sudden, and she leads us down this twisty chasm of a path, and the smoke thins slightly, and then we're in the cave, the one in the woods on the north side of the lake, the one where Zilpha and Felix were supposed to wait for the yellow dragon to show up.

We climb out of the hole and double over coughing.

"Come on!" Mom leads us back around the lake at a run, in the direction of the spy cabin. "We've got to get away from here. The smoke is still pretty thick."

She's right, of course, even though all I want to do is double over and cough and breathe. But the breathing won't do me any good until we get to fresh air, so Ed and I run and cough until suddenly, the ground gives this unsettling rumble and a jet like shooting fire erupts upward into the night from the direction of the cave.

I stop running and stare at the shooting jet of fire for a second, realizing Ed and I would have been shooting out of that hole *with* the fire had Mom not gotten us out of there.

Ed pulls me snug against his chest, his arms comforting around me. He's warm, which is nice, because in case you missed it, we're in Siberia in the middle of the night, and I'm not wearing much and I'm still damp from swimming through the lake.

"Let's get back to the spy cabin. Your father is going to be worried," Mom urges.

I hurry forward through the dark woods, holding tight to Ed's hand, not because I need him to help me find my way, but because I need the comfort of his touch.

"How did you know where to find us?" I ask Mom as we're running.

"The explosion lit up the cave and the lake simultaneously. That's when I suspected the two were connected. I ran in to look for Ed. I didn't even know you were in there."

"You went in to save Ed?" I'm panting, my lungs still not properly recovered from the smoky cave, but it feels good to force clear Siberian air through them, now that we're far enough from the smoke to breathe clearly.

"Yes. I was worried about him after the explosion."

Okay, maybe this is silly, but my mom's thoughtfulness and concern hit me in a tender spot. She went into the fiery cave—a place most safety-minded folks would widely avoid—to rescue Ed. And I don't have to ask why, because I know why. She cares about what happens to him because she knows I love him, and she loves me.

It hits me in little gasping waves, so that by the time we reach the spy cabin, my face is streaked with tears. Mom's about to run up the steps and inside, but I grab her sleeve and pull her back into a big hug.

"Thank you."

"For what?"

"For caring about Ed. For rescuing us from the exploding cave."

Mom hugs me back. "It's okay."

And then I realize something else—something important. "You know, you're pretty tough, for a mom."

Mom gives me a knowing look. "I'm a dragon. And what do you mean, *for a mom?* Our lives don't end when we have kids, any more than they end when we marry." Then she tweaks my cheek like I'm a little kid, because she's my mom and she can do that, and she hops up the steps and into the cabin.

Ed has been standing silently behind me this whole time. I turn and catch him smiling wryly. "Our lives don't end when we marry?" He repeats, his tone questioning.

"All the movies, you know," I shrug, feeling sheepish. "They always end when the couple falls in love and rides off into the sunset together. And I didn't want to end so I didn't want to get married." It sounds foolish, saying it out loud, now that I've realized it isn't true.

But Ed doesn't look at me like I'm a fool. He looks at me like he understands. "Aye, 'tis the great unknown. Would ye think less of me if I told ye, I was a bit skeered to leave Scotland with ye? Hadn't been off the island in many long years, not since yer grandmother Faye went missing, and I searched the world as best I could, but never found her. Felt the big world was just a place to get lost in, after that."

It's hard for me to imagine Ed being frightened of anything, considering how amazingly strong and brave he is. "Why did you go, then?"

211

"With you?" A smile spreads across his lips—a hunky kind of smile that makes me want to kiss him again. "Because ye let me. And I wanted to help. I wanted to be with ye." He dips his head toward mine. "I'd follow ye anywhere."

I'm tempted to kiss him again, but it's different this time, because it would be a real kiss, not just rescue breathing gone lovely. But there's more I need to say. "I think I'd follow you anywhere, too—since I kind of did, in the cave."

"How did ye get in the cave?" Ed asks.

"I jumped in the lake and swam through the tunnel."

Ed's eyes widen. "The lake was full of water yagi."

I shudder at the memory. "No kidding."

"But, yer more afeared of them than anythin'."

"I thought I was," I admit. "But it turns out, I'm more afraid of losing you. I—" My throat grows tight, and I look into Ed's emerald eyes. Dragon eyes are different from human eyes. The color is more vivid. They sort of glow. And sometimes, it's like we can talk to each other just with our eyes, communicating wordlessly whether we're in human or dragon form.

And right now, Ed's eyes are communicating a lot. That he loves me. That he's going to stand by me no matter what, that he'd swim through a lake thick with yagi and half electrocute himself for me. And that he's known, for a lot longer than I've been willing to admit it to myself, that I love him.

But I still feel like I need to say it out loud, because he said it out loud to me a long time ago, and that was brave of him, and I'd feel cowardly and unworthy of his love if I couldn't tell him how I feel. "I love you, Ed."

He grins. "I love you." And then he kisses me. A real, honest, non-rescue-breathing kiss. Ah, blissful.

"Now I can tell ye," he whispers part way through the kiss.

"Tell me what?"

"What yer mother and I talked about before we left Scotland."

It takes my kiss-muddled mind a moment to catch up. "What she told you? Oh, so you couldn't tell me until—"

"I promised her I wouldn't let on unless ye said ye loved me. Now that ye have, I can say what I know. Yer the one for me. It's more than love and feelin's. From the moment I caught yer scent, I knew ye were the one."

"But you didn't even know I was a dragon then. Did you?"

"I didn't know what I was smellin' or feelin' at first. 'Twas a befuddlement, indeed. Met many a female in my life, but none that drew me like ye. By the time I spoke with yer mother, I knew ye were a dragon, and that I'd wait as long as I had to, go anywhere, do anythin' to earn yer affection."

His speech stuns me to silence. I don't know how to respond. I just know it's been several long seconds, maybe even minutes, since my lips were on his.

That's too many minutes too long.

I wrap my arms around him and he pulls me close and kisses me again, and the night is no longer cold and my fears no longer frighten me.

Sure, there's a bunch of stuff I don't know, like whatever happened to my brothers when they flew off after that yellow dragon, or where Zilpha went when she and Jala were supposed to be watching the cave (seriously, I don't think anybody's seen Zilpha in hours) and where we're going to go from here and what Eudora's going to do. But I have a feeling all of that will sort itself out just fine.

I'm with Ed. And he's with me. Ed destroyed the water yagi machine *and* killed most of the water yagi on earth, which is far more than I'd have thought anyone could do.

And he did it for me.

THE END

A note from the author:

I hope you enjoyed *Hydra*. It's the second book in the Dragon Eye series. If you missed the first book, *Dragon*, I encourage you to read it, because it tells the story of how Ram and Ilsa got together, and introduces a bunch of things about dragons that might not be explained as well in later books.

There are four more books in the series after this one. The next is *Phoenix*. It follows Wren's little brother Felix on his adventures with the fiery yellow dragon. Please look for it and the rest of the Dragon books. If you enjoy these stories, please consider telling your friends about them, and leaving a review to let other readers know what you think.

Thank you for being a part of the dragon world.

While I'm being thankful, I'd like to extend my deepest gratitude to those people whose efforts and encouragement made this book possible. To Ray McCalla and Henry, for being some of my biggest and earliest supporters. To Stephany Matson and Colleen Burdsall, for their brilliant feedback, and to Virginia Munoz, who endured monstrous eyestrain to become one of the very first people to read the first book, and who, in doing so, has been a tremendous help and encouragement to me. Also to her children who, along with Eleanor and Genevieve, have become some of my best and youngest supporters.

And to all of you, Readers. You are a gift to me.
Finley